AN ALIEN
POKED ME

By Emma Jayne Taylor

Chapter One

Here I was, sat in my pokey little office on a Friday, trying to think of reasons to be grateful for having this shitty job. I guess I was more fortunate than those in the large, open partitioned spaces. The only thing I struggled with was the lonely separation. At least those having the stupid bit of hardboard separating their desks could speak to one another throughout the day. People feel awkward about knocking on my office door, but when they do it's only work-related bullshit. Maybe I was just hormonal today, or perhaps the poor weather was affecting my mood. I wouldn't be able to blame getting up on the wrong side of the bed. What a stupid saying. I usually get up on the same side anyway.

I appear to get a hell of a lot more work done than them lot out there who jabber too much. One thing advantageous to me is being able to play some low volume music for encouragement. I'm not sure if the big boss approves, but who gives a shit? I'm doing my job. Nobody has ever complained. I'm a great chief financial officer who worked my arse off to get where I am. Although I say that, I'm often growing bored with the same old churning away with figures and silly emails. Sometimes I feel like walking away and finding a simple life. I've paid my mortgage off and have plenty of savings. I guess that's the advantage of serious money management. I would look bad with the title I have if I was up to my eyeballs in debt!

I'm very young for all of this though. At 38 I still have some energy for the fun stuff.

Every evening I look forward to doing something a little more exciting. That's perhaps my telling sign that work is very boring. Sometimes you can have all the finances in the world and still find something missing in life. I think I've reached a point of recognising my need for internal happiness. Perhaps a bit more! At this point of thought, I decided I was going to stick to my contracted hours and stop with the extra time I seem to add on every day. I needed to find some life.

This was going to start today.

I stopped over analysing and picked some paperwork up that had been sat on the side for weeks on end. Going through it, I noticed it needed a heck of a lot of sorting out. This was good! My mind was seriously sucked into this now. Time moved faster, coffees slipped through my fingers and my music had played through automatically without being mindful of any of the tracks.

"Darn it!" I realised I had already broken my new mindful agreement to finish bang on time! It wasn't too disastrous however. I saved everything at a safe point for a plan of continuation on Monday and quickly logged off to grab my items. As I walked down the main corridor with my coat wrapped over my arm and handbag over one shoulder, I noticed some wondering eyes on me. I didn't think about the judgment some may have. Upon consideration, I realised that perhaps subconsciously I was working to the average leaving time of the majority. Perhaps this was out of sympathy. I grew cross with myself. I was one of the "top dogs".

"Jenny?" I heard my boss calling from the top end of the corridor that I had just abruptly left.
I spun to see him holding some forms, looking intent on asking some questions.
The usual, soft part of me nearly walked back to see what he needed, but my gut kicked into action.
"Oh, sorry James, have a nice weekend!"

Others were staring on but I didn't care as I walked confidently through the main office door and into the reception area.
"Goodnight Karen."
Even the receptionist was surprised to hear my words and see me walking firmly through the front doors.

Throwing everything into the passenger side of my car, I pondered over what I was going to do that was going to bring exciting change. It was a sudden feeling of an anti-climax.

Thinking about it, the bravest thing I have done for a number of years was simply leaving just past the official hours I was contracted to do. Now that is a boring-brave thing to do! Others would find bravery in walking out on a job completely, or heading off on an exotic holiday itinerary. Gosh I am boring! I need to do something out of this world! I had about twenty years to make up for. How did I get into this rut of boredom?

The first step in my mind was to head to a Public House on my own. I would pick up a good looking man and ask if he would consider something wild. I'm definitely not that way inclined, but if he was a respectable man, then he would also have some caution. Perhaps that was already a way of talking myself out of it. Why would I consider something wild and then add caution?

I decided the local Pub would definitely be something interesting as a start anyway.

"The Snowy Owl" - Sounded innocent. I could see a few business men heading there for their crafty post-work-beer before heading home.
I was nervous, but fought through the fear to order my drink at the bar. I didn't want to appear desperate, and I'm certain I didn't. I had sharp business clothes on and a bun of hair tightly wrapped on my head. Surely people would calculate my educated status. Recognising my thoughts, I suddenly realised how uptight I had become. I needed to find my inner humility and become more people focussed. Thankfully my hair is soft and silky, so I unravelled the tight bun to represent the literal "letting down of my hair."

"What can I get you?" An observant bar man noticed my awkward attempts to lighten myself up.
I could see his thoughts in his expressive eyes.
"Oh, could I have a plain orange juice please? I'm driving."
I was already apologising for my non-alcoholic drink.

Doubts quickly filled my mind as he nodded to fill the glass with a carton of pure orange juice. Perhaps this really wasn't me at all. Maybe I'm meant to remain my safe, boring collection of habits.

A kind looking gentleman stood beside me, holding a Five Pound Note, waiting to be served. He glanced over with an almost business-like smile.

"Just finished work?"

I guess that was the easiest way to start a conversation with someone looking the way I did. I observed his clothing to be of post-work status too.

"Yeah, I fancied a relaxed drink since it is Friday." I wasn't sure if I sounded casual enough.

"What do you do?"

"Ah just office work, you know?"

The bar man collected his payment and placed the drink delicately in front of me. He nodded to the man next to me.

"Usual Sir?"

Realising the man beside me was a regular to this; I wondered how unnatural I looked to him.

I was an alien to regular pub time. An odd meal, or ladies' chat perhaps, but this was uncomfortable.

After the drinks were served, the kind man took his and walked over to a large table full of other well-dressed men. I tried not to keep my eyes there and pondered uncomfortably, wondering why I decided to try this move in the first place. I could have called a friend to head out with. *That* was safe.

This safe and boring lifestyle reminded me of the need to be wild. But how wild was I thinking? This place wasn't short of people, but they were all engrossed in their groups or partners. This reminded me of how quiet my life truly is.

I felt embarrassed about being on my own and considered leaving.

All of a sudden I felt my mobile phone vibrating in my bag. A faint ring helped me to demonstrate that I wasn't attempting to answer a fake call in order to look more popular. I reached in.

"Hello?" I was comforted by a friend calling.

"Jenny, are you still at work?"

"Hi Karen, I guess I would normally be, but I left a bit earlier being a Friday."

Karen is a long term friend who always checks in on me regularly, but this was perfecting timing.

"Are you at home then?" She checked.

"Actually, I came to a local pub. I don't know what I'm thinking. Ha!"

"On your own?" She obviously filled in the blanks.

"Yeah, I just fancied it."

"Oh wow, that's brave. I was just wondering if you were doing the Yoga tonight. If you were I could pick you up on the way through. I decided to go straight from work, so it's closer."

I paused. I wasn't really in the mood for Yoga. I thought I'd be honest.

"Ah, I think I'll probably miss it tonight. I'm not really in the mood for it. I hope you don't mind. Can Kerry go if you need company?"

It was as if I could hear Karen's thoughts. I haven't missed a Yoga class for about ten years. This would be a shock to her ears!

"Oh, well, yes; I'm sure Kerry will be there. If you really don't fancy it, then I'm sure we can catch up next week."

"Great. I could pick you up if you like?" The guilt was shining through, obviously.

"Okay. Well, enjoy whatever you're up to in the pub. Tell me all about it when we catch up."

"Sure will my lovely. Take care for now."

"See you then. Bye."

"Bye."

It felt awkward. Our conversation usually flowed and the plans were always very rigid and expected. Everything has been predictable up to now. It was time to break the chain. My friends care enough for me to know that I can talk to them about anything at any time. This was just an urge to live differently, with just a little bit more fun.

As I put the phone away, a couple of bantering men were laughing at each other as they approached the bar. I drank as if to demonstrate I was in my own little world, despite having all of the self- awareness in the world.

They both stopped and looked over at me. I felt it, but also noticed it in my peripheral vision.

"Hello sweetie. Did you want something a little stronger?"

The question was cheap and tacky, but with the way I was feeling, I was open to a different type of conversation. Perhaps I wanted to feel younger again. I looked at them and gave a friendly smile. "I'm okay thank you. I need to drive after this."

They both looked a bit perplexed. One of them openly asked why I would sit at a bar, evidentially after work, just to drink something non-alcoholic. I didn't feel the need to have to explain myself, but I found myself doing it anyway!

"I just felt like being in a different scene after work today. I'm driving, but not big on drinking anyway."

One of the men looked a little more reserved than the other. He looked as if he understood more.

"I get that. I get dragged here at times. I'm not big on drinking. I guess it's just for the social aspect."

He sounded more intelligent than his impression gave. I looked at him for a while, longer than perhaps I should have. I noticed his soft features, but a very well styled haircut. I liked it, so looked on again. His friend noticed my focus and looked back and forth between us. He attempted to break any potential advance by confirming the drink request with him.

They soon had their drinks served and walked further away. I noticed the cute bodies in their jeans and trendy shirts. They must have been a similar age to me, but it was hard to tell. They still looked relatively young, but had that more mature action about them.

I felt weird about the brief conversation and wondered if I was giving the wrong impression. My little silver watch showed I had been there for a little less than an hour and I was already keen to leave. Perhaps that Yoga lesson could still be made.

As if the two young men had noticed my plan to go, the soft-faced one gestured kindly for me to join them. I very nearly left anyway, as the thought to join them seemed nerve wracking! Perhaps a little company for a short time would make this visit feel a little more worthwhile. I started to make my way over. They pushed a chair out with a foot. Almost enough to call it traditional gentlemanly behaviour... Almost!

I pulled it further to get my long legs in. I always thought my legs were a great feature.

The other man had a heavy set of stubble around his mouth and appeared to be more confident about himself. I wasn't sure what kind of situation I was getting into, but the one thing to be confident about was the fact that I was in a place full of many others. I felt relatively safe in this particular pub. I looked over at the bar man and noticed his head lift to gesture a hello. It comforted me to know that he was the observant type. I had my fair share of blind dates and set-ups enough to feel relatively comfortable about talking to two strangers.

I should have predicted the first question after joining them.

"So why is a pretty girl sat on her own in a big pub?"

I didn't know whether to demonstrate my intellect with a mention of predictability, or to play the squirmy innocent girl. Strangely I found myself grinning respectfully without a word. I couldn't seem to reply. I took another sip of my orange juice! The soft faced man introduced them finally.

"So, this is Chris and I'm Jack."

"Nice to meet you," I grinned and paused, offering a slightly longer sentence, "So, I came here to relax after work with a non-alcoholic drink."

The men gave a light chuckle under their breath.

"Relaxing with an orange juice," Chris just couldn't let it go, but it became the repeated joke for him.

We spoke with the usual build-up of small talk first. I discovered they both worked in construction which is where their close friendship developed.

After some time I noticed that Chris wasn't such a tough guy after all. He had normal conversation about him. They admitted I broke their usual boring conversation, and *I* admitted they helped me break my boredom of the usual routine.

Chris looked at Jack and stated it was time for him to head home. Apparently he had a couple of young children and a dinner to get back to. That was nice to hear, although I wasn't sure if it was a deliberate move to leave Jack and I alone, but it was nice anyway. Jack and I spoke for about another hour before I mentioned that I should make my merry way. He touched my hand and asked me to stay a little longer. I foolishly made an excuse about having to get back to feed a neighbour's dog. What a chicken I am!

"Will you call me if I give you my number?" This certainly confirmed his like for me.

"Of course, you're very nice."

I wasn't expecting anything other than for him to organise his phone to the contact list, but he surprised me by leaning in and giving me a very soft kiss on my cheek. I felt all gooey and honoured. He must have noticed my positive reaction instantly, as he reached in for a good kiss on the lips. I was quite taken aback, but went with it. He gently actioned for a longer kiss and I naturally complied. Before I knew it, we were kissing wildly, holding and rubbing one another's necks. I wanted something wild, but felt new to this. It had been too many years since feeling this way. He paused to speak.

"Are you sure we can't feed the dog together?"

I felt nervous about his obvious desire. I didn't normally offer myself on a plate on the first date!

"Okay, I confess, there is no dog."

"So you just wanted to get away?"

We still retained our gentle grip on each other's necks.

Well, I just don't think it's a good idea to jump into bed on a first date that I wasn't truly expecting. I didn't even expect this nice kissing, as we've only just met!

"We obviously have chemistry. Do you feel I wouldn't respect you?"

"No, I just feel it is disrespectful to myself."

He looked wise in his eyes upon hearing my words.

"I get that."

The words he used when we first spoke. It was cute.

"Let me take you to your car then at least."

"Gentlemanly."

As we walked, I was so tempted to continue on my wild quest and invite him to mine.

We reached my car and he kissed me very seductively again.

When he came up for air, he asked if we could do the number exchange.

Like a show-off, I reached into my purse and pulled out a business card. I noticed his grin, but light disappointment in his eyes.

"I'm sorry, it's a habit. I didn't mean to flaunt my assets, or be so business-like."

"Well, I prefer the flaunting of other assets."

I walked into that one.

"If you call me, we could get to know one another a lot more if you like?"

"Okay, I respect you for not jumping into bed with a stranger. I do find you very attractive though."

"I find you gorgeous."

We grinned at one another and had one final kiss before I slipped into my driver's seat and gently closed the door.

I didn't want to drag the situation out anymore, so I started the engine and gently reversed. He waved with his other hand in his pocket, trying to look relaxed.

So much for wild! Did I buck out of my daring plans? I'm sure I don't want to behave like some kind of sleaze.

I pressed the dash for some music and turned it up to a high volume. The roads seemed quiet, so I put my foot down harder on the accelerator. I took corners sharply and raced hard up the inclines. Thoughts of still catching the Yoga session passed, but then I'd be cutting it fine and would need to change clothes. The wild plans seemed to be cut short.

As I drove, I thought long and hard about how I would make small changes to enhance my fun in life. I decided I would write down everything I ever wanted to do, but never seemed to find time for.

My house is a decent home. I drove up the driveway, pulling into the electrically raised door of the garage. I crawled out of the car and walked calmly into a side door internally, leading into my kitchen. I was feeling grateful for my home. I wouldn't want to wreck it by acting drastic in any shape or form, such as walking out of work, but I really did just want to do some fun, wild things.

Placing my handbag on one of the worktops, I noticed the glare of my mobile phone. Several people had sent messages. There was a missed call from my boss, James. I noticed a voicemail. This seemed to be the sign of someone who was discouraged by my early departure. It was annoying to think that my boss was encouraging longer hours than I was employed to do. I refused to listen to the voicemail he obviously left for me.

So what now? Was that it for my wild time?

Ah, where is that note pad?

I made a note of everything - things big and small. After a while I felt silly. Perhaps this was a midlife crisis. I'm sure I was too young for that however. I wondered if an overdue holiday may do me some good. The message from my boss came to mind again. If he is sympathetic, then perhaps I could request a short-noticed break and get all of my desires out of my system within a couple of weeks. The urge to be wild was just digging away at me, but I needed to keep logical too.

It would be silly to risk everything.

I caved in and reluctantly listened to the voicemail.

"Hi Jenny, we were all concerned with you suddenly walking away. I'm just checking all is okay with you. Give me a call when you're safely home."

I felt a bit angry for wondering why I shouldn't be able to walk away once my hours were done. The sympathy was there to be taken advantage of however.

I took a deep breath and hit James' contact number. The answer was pretty much immediate!

"Hi Jenny."

"Hi, I heard your voicemail. I'm sorry if I seemed to be abrupt in my departure, but I fancied leaving at the time I am contracted to, today. I am starting to feel frustrated about not having the work-life balance as of late. I don't know why this has suddenly hit me."

I felt as if I was talking very robotically, attempting to spill everything within one breath. I worried that he may suspect I had a prepared speech. It felt silly, as James and I know each other very well having worked very closely for many years.

He did appear to be reading my mind.

"There's no need to be official with me. Let's talk off-the-books. Did you need some time off? I can't remember the last time you took any holiday."

"Well, it's funny you should ask that, as I wondered if that was all I needed. Is it a good time to take a couple of weeks though?"

"Hey, not a lot's going on, so please, take some time and come back when you get bored."

"Really? I can do that?"

I heard him breathing with a slight panic, as if he could hear too much excitement from my voice.

"Well, I don't think any more than two weeks to start with. I assume you will get bored only because of your very active mind and your usual drive to get things done."

"Thanks James. I accept the holiday as of today and plan to return with a fresh and positive attitude."

"That's what I want to hear! I'll see you soon then. Enjoy yourself."

We said our goodbyes and I was surprised with the instant results. Perhaps we can have anything we wish for. I have read many books on manifesting and the law of attraction, but never put the information into action.

I decided I would begin by having that second date and start putting some other exciting plans together.

Chapter Two

I woke with a little bit of apprehension, since I didn't have my usual routine to adhere to.

"Get up!" I shouted at myself and flung my legs to the side of the bed.

I slowly gathered myself and put a humorous radio station on to get my mood up for the day. The mobile phone was buzzing with too many messages again. I sifted through them to find one from Jack.

"Hi Sexy, I wondered when I would get to see you again. You have my number now.-Jack."

Ooh, exciting!

At least I made a good-enough impression for him to get in touch. I worried he'd see straight into my usually-boring brain. I wonder if he would still like me if I had my usual routine.

I returned a text.

"Hey you! I can meet anytime you are free. Thanks for your number. X"

Did I sound boring? He started with "Hi sexy", but here I am with plain old words.

I looked on at other messages and discovered a couple of friends had missed me from the Yoga class. My great friend asked if I was free for a catch-up at hers.

I realised my first day had no exciting plans whatsoever. I needed to get the fun things organised. The day started with the boring chores that needed doing.

Randomly, a little later, I decided to walk to a local forest and go for a gentle jog. The headphones were on and my body was pumped. Some older people were walking by, glaring at me as if I was committing some kind of crime! I ran on with a faster pace. After a good half an hour, I slowed my pace and decided to cool down for a pleasant walk. It was always very good for me to recognise that I could still run for a while non-stop. I don't like the fitness levels to drop.

I looked down at my phone to see that Jack was hoping to meet up after he'd finished work. I thought about how gross it would be to offer him the sight of my body in the sweaty state that it currently was!

Jack was able to leave work early, by three o'clock in the afternoon, so I rushed home to have a thorough shower, getting into every crack! I looked on at myself in the mirror and admired my pert breasts.
I've still got it!

I thought about taking a photo of myself for hindsight. Time was going by so fast that I will one day need to smile at the wonderful figure that I had!

Stuff it. I took a photo using my phone. It was a great photo, one to always look back on.

I put too much perfume on. It irritated my nose and breathing passages. I coughed a few times and got dressed into a low-cut, attractive top and a tight pair of leggings. I wanted to say "sexy", but not "slutty."

Jack was waiting for me in the same pub, on his own this time. I met him at the same table. I couldn't help but think I didn't want *this* to become the same routine!

He stood when he saw me and walked over to give me a gentle welcoming peck on the lips. He must have smelt me, as he apologised for his post-work aroma.

"You look amazing!" He looked down at my chest area.

"Thank you."

"So, did you want to have a drink here? Or did you fancy a different scene?"

Thank goodness for his options! I didn't fancy the same view as the first date. The worry of repetition not being good for me at this period in time crossed my mind initially. I felt as if I'd moved up a notch in my desire to have some fun.

I thought for a moment.

"Let's head out somewhere."

I noticed his smile of approval.

"I know this neat place."

We left in his construction van. It didn't feel very romantic initially and thoughts crossed my mind that I didn't know this man very well, but he seemed to be a good hearted man.

It wasn't far down the road that we came to a dirt track that brought us to a large grass mound with a path cutting directly through it.

"Let me show you this pretty place."

I felt nervous but excited at the same time. He noticed my nervousness and gently touched my hand.

"It's okay, you can trust me. It's just a natural place of beauty – a pretty walk."

I breathed out, not realising my lungs were holding air for quite some time with slight fear.

We walked over the grass mound and landed into an area with a long track circling around a large lake. In the distance appeared to be a mini castle, with tumbling rubble all around it.

"How come I haven't seen this place before?" I was impressed.

"I love this little piece of escape when things can get on top of me, mostly with work."

I enjoyed the scene before my eyes and took in his words, wondering if he was a sensitive kind of man.

We walked for at least an hour. The sun was just warm enough to allow comfort.

He took us into the surrounds of an old structure that reminded me of a castle. Old rock held together to form different levels in height, creating a pretty good building structure to hide in. It was interesting to see, but I didn't know anything about it. When I asked Jack where we were, he didn't even know himself. He told me that he'd found it accidentally one day when he needed to rush into a private area for a wee!

This space of rubble allowed inventive chairs to sit on. Jack sat on a comfortable level of rubble and I decided to surprise him. I sat on his lap and gave him an encouraging kiss. He complied with my physical desires and we fondled for a long time, moving to different areas, retaining privacy in this seemingly-secret space. I noticed him looking through the cracks of the old parts of the building to check for privacy.

He entered me before I even realised his plan. I removed a condom from my handbag with my free arm. He grinned and quickly placed it on correctly, re-entering and moving vigorously in and out. We both reached our peak at the same time and let out our natural pleasure calls. At this point we didn't care if anyone was about, as we were completely in the moment.

Just as Jack was gathering his normal thoughts, we heard a crunch underfoot outside. We swiftly put ourselves together, but not quickly enough! A man, all in green was fiddling with his phone, trying to either make a swift call or prepare to take a photo or video of us. We also heard the crackle of a hand held security radio, causing us to look at each other with extremely frightened eyes!

Jack looked over to an opposite opening and gave a head signal to move swiftly. He grabbed my hand and we ran like the wind, stumbling over our feet as we did our best to escape the scene.

Jack said he caught eye of a park-ranger type person stood by the side of the rubble, looking on at us running, not able to get any of his equipment to do the effective capturing thing. All he could manage was a distant shout.

"Hey!"

We ran and ran, until we reached the van, which we prayed hadn't been taken note of. There was no time to grab our breath or cool down from the long sprint. All that was in sight was to get the engine running and to speed off as swiftly as possible.

We chuckled and swore all the while, as the van was moving down the open road. Jack suddenly said something that made me think.

"I have never found such a fun, adventurous lady before. You could be my perfect soul mate."

I felt a sudden panic fill me, thinking I was giving him the alternate version of myself. I wasn't sure if this was the real me breaking out, but I realised this was extremely great fun.

He looked over at me, noticing my expression.

"Are you okay?"

"Oh heck yes! That was fun!"

Relief filled his face and a great questioning time of my own mind was about to fill me.

That night, after our goodbyes and separations, we sat in our own abodes. Thankfully it gave me time to ponder over the day. I realised it opened a new gate in my mind. All this time, others are probably leading this exciting action, with daring opportunities, when I'm normally working and continuing with the boring routines day by day. My youth contained the fun and excitement that today reminded me of, but as I've aged, it has gradually faded. Most of my friends are family orientated, full of kids and extremely busy lives and all I have done is consumed myself mostly with heavy duty office work.

I took my list of fun things to do and ticked by the side of my completed actions. Today was close to a high speed police chase, so I took it as that. Some of the romantic scenes were marked off. I was laughing at some of the ridiculous ideas I had.

Tomorrow I wanted to try my hand at ice skating. I remembered trying it as a kid, but only for a short spate of time. I thought a friend may wish to join me, but after texting everyone I considered, they all decided it was too dangerous for them. Fear of severed fingers, or injured bottoms were communicated to me in great detail. It occurred to me that maybe all of my surrounding acquaintances and friends were working on my usual level of safe and boring routine. I decided I would still be giving it my all.

I went to bed that night with a huge smile, giggling occasionally at the risky adventure today had brought.
It was surprising that I even had the calm to go to sleep, but I drifted into a deep state rather swiftly.

The following morning I woke to several messages on the mobile phone from Jack. It felt an inconvenience to start with, but after reading a couple, they were brief and continuous (short, sharp messages that lead onto the next and the next). It was nice to see that I had a wonderful impact on him.

As I gradually put myself together for the day, I still wanted to put my feet into ice skates and give it a go. I realised this was something I needed to do myself.
With not wanting to waste the day, I hopped into the car and drove towards the local ice rink. I had passed this venue many times and wondered what it would be like to take part in the events they often had. For a moment, I felt like a child dreaming for my mother to be with me to get me started. I shook my head, telling myself I needed to do this the adult way!

I walked in, paid for my single ticket; picked up the boots, putting them on awkwardly. It was fun to watch others struggling to put theirs on or take them off. Some looked very experienced and others looked as if they'd also had a spontaneous idea for giving this a go.
Perhaps I should be keeping a diary to replace my list.
"Day Number two: Trying my hand... losing my hand... err, no! I must remain optimistic."
I corrected my thoughts and watched for others literally slipping into the rink through the doorway. The circular skating looked enjoyable. Thankfully there weren't many attending today. Perhaps I should have invited Jack! We didn't make any follow-

up plans, but I didn't want to overkill our initial dates. Perhaps he fancied a relaxing Sunday anyway. I was yet to reply to his messages. Keep him guessing for a little while... I felt like a teenager with my thoughts, as I nervously started walking on the carpet towards the ice rink.

I suddenly became very self-aware and carefully placed one foot on the ice. I looked up at everyone else moving at super speed. I couldn't let go of the wall, as I placed both feet on the ice and scuffled along. I tried to put my mind back to my cool roller skating days and associate it with this act. It worked as I gradually grew confidence and let go of the wall. The speed and excitement was fantastic! I was back in my childhood mind, zooming around and picking up tips and tricks by observing others. I knew how to stop suddenly and could just about skate backwards.

After rushing around for a while and really feeling the buzz, I noticed a young man trying to pass me on the inside of the circle several times. I ignored him, thinking he was just showing off or being an idiot. After the fifth consecutive time he made things really obvious with a cheeky smile and glimmering eyes. My ego was buzzing now! Maybe I needed to regain my confidence as a woman. This holiday was certainly helping me in *that* way so far.

After what felt like a few hours, I stumbled back onto normal ground and found my legs were like lead! I almost fell over, stumbling over to a bench to change back into my normal shoes. The young man who had been circling beside me made his obvious move. He came to sit next to me, declaring a sudden coincidence for being there at the same time. The cheesiness of it made me feel uncomfortable.

"Oh, hello there! You're the one I skated close to for a while."

His facial expression was so dramatized.

I smiled and let out a small mutter that was too honest.

"Uh."

I was struggling to get out of the tight boot laces and wondered how many people had worn the same boots over the years. I knew I had the average sized foot. These thoughts made me realise how uninterested I was with the interruptive company. He surprised me with a question.

"So have you skated long?"

I really didn't want to waste either of our times, so my words may have seemed a little bit harsh.

"Look, I have a boyfriend, so I really don't want you to waste your time."

"Oh! No! I am just being friendly. I do apologise if I made you feel uncomfortable."

The return tone-of-voice made me feel guilty, which forced me to look up into his eyes after putting my own shoes on comfortably. What I saw made me feel like eating my previously rude words! His eyes were a piercing blue, yet were quite deep set under very strikingly tidy, manly eyebrows. His eyes made me look further, and so I inspected his perfect dark hair and chiselled features. His chest was firm and strong looking and his shoulders wide. I couldn't help but look further down to his flat abs and toned legs. I couldn't believe the perfectly modelled man was talking to someone like me!

"Ah, look, I'm really sorry. I really didn't mean to sound rude. I suppose I assumed you were hitting on me. I am kind-a single, but, you know a girl has to protect herself."

I felt as if fresh dribble was falling from my lips. A fresh grin filled his face, causing genuine lines under his eyes.

"Well, I was caught up with your long legs and couldn't help but come and see who owned them."

I certainly hadn't heard that line before, but the beautiful aura around him just sucked me in. I talked to myself inside.

He may be attractive, but you'd get so sick of his obvious lines. Come on, you prefer some intellectual conversation. This would just be a bit of fun... Ooh, a bit of fun? No! No! I can't make this holiday all about slutty stuff. I am not a tart! The outdoor sex was already out of character. No, No!

"Hey, was that the wrong thing to say? I hope I haven't upset you."

I didn't realise my eyes were tightly shut with my thoughts.

"Oh no, you're fine. I mean, you're great. This is the first time I've ice skated, so it was all trial and error."

His gorgeous smile beamed and my logical side just melted.

"Are you tired? Did you want to grab a quick drink to refresh with me?"

Oh gosh. How obvious can he be? Maybe I could just stare at his face for a little while. Just for a bit.

I agreed and we both walked over to return our boots before heading off to the leisure centre's canteen area.

Classy.

I couldn't help feel snobby about the choice of places to get to know someone. He seemed worth it though.

We exchanged the usual conversation... What we did for a living; what hobbies we had; where we lived and what music taste we might have shared. Although my mind was bored, I couldn't stop admiring his extremely good looks.

His name was Jason, he worked as a retail manager; a lover of all sports, sharing the same variety of music that I did... Apparently!

Then it suddenly struck me. I was being a fool! Why would such a good looking man want to chat with me in a cheap café? How many times has he done this with his cheesy lines and his sexy smile? I'm one of his easy lays!

"So how come someone as handsome as you isn't married already with kids?" I just couldn't hold back on that question.

I heard him sigh and noted the drop of his eyelids.

"The truth is I keep meeting the wrong kind of ladies. They tend to use me for my looks, almost as if they need me to be their trophy. After a few dates I tend to get dumped. They usually give me the line of needing someone they can relax with. Apparently the punishment I receive for being good looking is that they feel the pressure to remain high maintenance for me. I don't care how a lady looks. It's just important to have a wonderful connection. I have the right to be happy too."

Wow, he certainly let a lot of feelings out in one hit!

I felt as if I was suddenly connecting with him. A further question however puzzled me.

"So, then how do you have the confidence to pick up someone like me, just like that?"

"I noticed your kind face and your delicate skate. That might sound strange, but I can tell a lot from the way someone skates. Skating is a regular event for me. I see lots of people's skills and movements. It was clear that you were new to it all, but you built up such an amazing amount of confidence in a short space of time. Your legs looked so elegant. I couldn't help but stare at you."

"You knew it was my first time? I thought I did well at hiding that." I chuckled.

"I know I used a rubbish chat-up line with asking how long you'd been skating for, but when I get nervous I say stupid things."

Oh jeepers! This guy is turning things around. I may have misjudged him entirely. Give him some time!

I stared at this man, wondering if he was as genuine as he seemed. My gut instinct was telling me of his innocence.

We spoke for ages and ended up ordering some food to cover the hungering lunch time pangs. I couldn't believe the time when I looked down at my delicate silver watch.

"Oh my! I really need to get going!"

His face dropped.

"Ah, I'm sorry. I didn't even ask if you had time to talk for this long. I'm free of work this week."

"Are you on holiday too then?"

"Yes. I really needed a week of just doing nothing."

"Lovely!" I didn't want to admit to having even more free time than that.

"So I feel we got on extremely well. If you have-to go then could we possibly exchange numbers?"

Oh gosh, this is becoming a habit! Collecting men's numbers! He was so polite in his asking that I couldn't refuse. We added each other's contact details into our phones, had a polite hug and said our goodbyes.

I didn't give any excuses for my sudden departure, but was prepared to give the "dog reason" if I panicked!

I later sat in my car, wondering if I should be the tart-role I seem to be playing out lately and allow myself to date both of the men for a while until one captures my heart. *Fun!* I reminded myself of the planned venture of fun. It would be difficult trying to remember what I told each one, so perhaps I should attempt to keep the same stories for both.

I'll just be myself. So...What's next?

I felt as if I was on a roll, but wanted to do something completely different.

Hmm, Sunday, Sunday... I can't go drinking too much and I've exercised enough for one day.

I decided I would at least ask my friends if they fancied a relaxing few drinks at mine. It's a rarity to have guests with my usually boring routines.

Within minutes, I managed to accumulate three other friends for a get-together of drinks and nibbles, over a mushy black and white movie. They all sounded surprised over the invite.

I was surprised to hear that they would do it considering it was extremely short notice.

On my route home, I picked some cheap drink and nibbles up. Crisps and nuts work well, but the chocolate was a must!

Before I knew it, Karen, Kerry and Claire made their way over and jumped into their comforts on my spacious sofa. I had the perfect space for guests and parties, yet kept it all selfishly to myself. This annoyed me, but I threw those thoughts out, ready to enjoy some lady chuckles.

We didn't really watch the movie someone had candidly selected. We all chuckled, ate and drank abundantly. I felt very happy. I'm not sure if it was the alcohol, but I recognised my need for friends and interaction.
The drink flowed and some board games were beginning to take place, with loud music in the background. I knew my head was beginning to spin, as this music seemed more distant as time went along. We all found extreme laughter over something that seemed vague. Karen took her phone out and began filming our crazy laughter, as we stupidly flaunted ourselves, perhaps a teasing bra strap slipping down provocatively. It all felt wonderfully stupid.

I didn't remember much after our extreme chuckles, but know I was comfortable on a long stretch of my sofa.

My head must've fallen back, as I woke the following morning sat perfectly upright with a slightly spilt glass still sitting in my hand. I looked around to note bits of food on the floor and too many glasses scattered all over the place. Considering there was only a gathering of four people, the place looked completely trashed.

As I moved slowly, I felt the stiffness of my neck and dryness of my mouth. I couldn't recall the ladies' departure. In fact, I needed to inspect the place.

"Hello?" I got up and walked around, going into each bedroom and back to the lounge and kitchen.

There were literally no "bodies" lying around much to my relief! I looked in the mirror and I was a wreck. Make-up was smeared wonderfully all over my cheeks. My clothing was half on, with one arm sleeve hanging halfway down my arm and I was adamant I must have changed my trousers, as these were very loose tracksuit bottoms, which I certainly didn't have on when the ladies came initially. I tried to recall our events. It was then a concern that my friends had perhaps left in a taxi late at night, or decided to leave early in the morning. With these thoughts, I needed to get to my mobile phone. I eventually found it between the seats of the sofa and noted several missed messages and calls. I threw it back on the sofa, thinking it was more important to get my head straight.

A soothing shower felt so wonderful. I have never appreciated the feeling of the water trickling over my head and body so much in my entire life. I instantly felt more alive. I decided to stay in a bath robe for a few hours and get some food and water into my system. The phone was constantly 'pinging', but I couldn't stand the thought of looking at the bright screen with my sensitive eyes.

All I fancied doing was relaxing and recovering. I realised there had been too many years of avoiding this feeling by attending Yoga, the gym and forcing myself to run and take part in various sports. I was beginning to think it must be good to occasionally let my hair down.

I eventually took note of my phone as I sat on the sofa. The first thing I noticed was the amount of missed calls. Jack, Jason, Karen and Kerry had all tried several times. I began to wonder if something bad may have happened, but hoped it was just to review our mad night. With instinct I called Karen first, since we were closest. She answered on the first ring!

"Hi Jenny, I'm so sorry! I really didn't mean to get us so messed up!"

Her voice sounded very stressed, but I attempted to ease her mind.

"How can it be *your* fault? We all made our individual choices on the drink. It was fun. Please don't tell me you had as much as me, but have gone into work!"

There was quite a surprisingly long pause.

"You mean you don't know what I'm talking about?"

It was my turn to pause with lack of understanding. Concern built up.

"I take it everyone got back to safety?"

"Jenny, I'm really sorry. Somehow one of our videos was uploaded and before I knew about it, the views were off the charts. I've obviously removed it now, but I can't remember doing it! I don't know who's seen it, but it had over two million hits!"

I thought and wondered what the problem was, but my hair was standing up in slight fear by the sound of her voice.

"Well... What was the video about? I remember messing around with a bit of flirting."

"You can't recall?" Karen sounded even more concerned.

"I really can't."

The silence worried me again for a moment.

"Well, the others found it funny, but their husbands weren't too happy. I guess time will allow people to forget. I'm just glad you don't have to answer to anyone. I'm just worried about what your boss would think."

"What the hell are you talking about Karen? Please give me some detail!"

"Sorry. I really thought you were still aware of things. You must've drunk a bit too much. We left you at around one o'clock as you fell asleep. Claire's man came to take us all home. We didn't bring any sleeping gear. It wasn't meant to have gone as far as it went."

I waited for her to continue.

"You see, we were doing some silly flaunting in front of my recording phone. I was having an innocent chuckle, but I uploaded one that was showing too much of our bits. Everyone was egging me on to do it, so I did. I was just as drunk as the others, but I wasn't thinking straight. I didn't realise we exposed so much!"

I sucked in a big gasp of air once I recalled snippets of the memory.

"Oh no! I think we were all stripping and kissing... Oh no! We were all fondling each other and throwing our clothes on the floor!"

"You remember?" Karen sounded slightly relieved.

"I remember bits. That explains my different trousers."

I began to laugh slightly, but Karen remained serious.

"It's okay isn't it?"

There was a moment of silence and I couldn't imagine the reason behind it. It worried me slightly.

"Well, it's upset Kerry's husband. They're having some issues. I'm praying it will all blow over though."

"Ah no, I thought *some* liked watching others."

"Well, he does seem a bit like a down-to-Earth kind-a guy I guess."

"Maybe we did take it too far."

"I can remember some crazy scenes!" Karen began to follow through with a laugh, which helped me relieve some tension.

"I guess we may all be feeling a bit tender today as well. Time has to be the answer."

I thought for a moment and realised the potential disaster!

"Oh shit! James! And everyone at work!"

"Well, that's what I was worrying about too."

I realised Karen had more time to be ahead of the game.

"Oh shit. I've kind of started seeing someone too!"

I didn't let on that I was actually dating a couple of men. She may be a close friend, but there are still some morals to be demonstrating.

Karen and I spoke for some time about potential disasters surrounding the video. We calmed over time, realising our partial paranoia. It was time to slowly say our goodbyes.

Upon leaving the call I checked the other notifications on the phone.
In order of arrival, I noticed Karen and Kerry had called first, and several times. Jack had attempted to call me several times. Jason attempted to call just the once. It wasn't as dramatic as I first thought.
I moved to the text messages and Jack was only asking for me to get in touch as it had been a while since hearing from me. Kerry sent one that simply said:
"We are in deep doo-doo."
Jason had also left one saying he'd like to meet up again, as he really enjoyed our chat. Huge relief hit me, knowing I hadn't ruined my date potentials.

Time slipped by as I relaxed for a while. Although I didn't get to see the video, it was just crazy fun in *my* head, and despite that, it has been deleted. Those who enjoyed watching it would have had a short minute or two of pleasure I'm sure!
Kerry's relationship will repair itself. I was certain that her husband would feel less insecure in good time. At the end of the day it was just a bit of girly fun!

I stood up to find some more hydration from the kitchen. I remembered how tired I felt after the crazy night. It was good just to relax anyway.

It was nice to loaf around without any fancy hairstyle or make-up on the face. After grabbing a drink from the kitchen, I sat comfortably and switched some rubbish television on to literally stare at.

After only a very short while of relaxing, the doorbell rang. I jolted and hoped it was just a cold caller. My house is large, so I couldn't see far enough down the corridor to see any clues of body shape or face recognition through the small, designer glass panels that were dotted around the door.

I whispered for them to go away, but the person hit the doorbell three times in a row. All sorts of fearful thoughts flew through my mind at this point. I wondered if someone was kindly warning me of something. Nobody visited without arrangements normally, so this was odd. It was annoying to think that the intercom system I wanted to install wasn't fitted months ago when I was contemplating it.

When the bell went again, I thought "shit" and rose to face the music. Upon opening the door, I noticed the sight of one of my neighbours. Flashes of memories went through my mind as I automatically asked what the problem was. I would usually see this person washing his car, or mowing his lawn, flaunting his perfectly formed chest and bottom. As I spoke, I felt my temperature rise in embarrassment.

"Your car Madam," was all he mustered up, as he pointed to the scene.

I reached my messy head through the door, to see that someone had kindly spray painted some words on the sides and bonnet.

SLEEZY BITCH

CHEAP SLAG

TART

I looked at the words in horror! The first culprit that came to mind was Kerry's husband.

I must have looked shocked and disturbed, as my neighbour was speaking with concern.

"Are you okay Ma'am? I can help you wash it off. You must have upset someone badly. I wasn't sure if you knew about it or not. I don't normally see your vehicle outside. I thought you always worked. I'm sure I can help you get it off."

His voice had a slight accent to it. Although I was shocked, I was picking such little, unimportant things up like that.

Other thoughts shot through my mind such as being so foolish to have drunk so much.

"Ma'am? Do you need to sit down? Maybe I could grab you a coffee or something, help you relax. Leave the fixing of your car to me."

I realised how bad I must have looked.

"Oh, I am okay, err, sorry, I realise I don't actually know your name."

"Patrick Ma'am."

This man was too polite!

"Oh please call me Jenny. My name is Jenny."

"Thank you Jenny."

Again, too polite!

"Well, Patrick, I am so grateful that you came over to tell me about the car." I needed to probe. "Do you know who might have done it? Did you see any strange behaviour at any time?"

"Oh, no Ma'am; I mean, Jenny. I just came downstairs to notice your car was out, which is not your usual habit. When I looked for longer than a moment, I noticed the words on it."

I noticed how sweet this man was. It was difficult to hold confidence about myself when I recalled how bad my physical appearance must have been at this moment.

"I, err, had a few drinks with some ladies last night. They were picked up by one of their partners. We didn't disturb you did we?"

He seemed surprised. "Oh no, I slept like a baby. It was just now, when I looked out to notice your car that I noticed something was weird."

I must have let out an obvious, disappointing sigh.

"Let me clean your car up for you. I will be happy for just a coffee and chat afterwards."

For an instant, I worried that this could potentially become the third instalment of "tarty" actions.

"Oh, I can pay you for your work. It would be very kind of you."

Patrick looked uncomfortable. "I have plenty of money my-lady; it is just to help you in this time. I am good with car things and paintwork."

I couldn't believe his polite words and kindness.

"My goodness, well I would be ever so grateful. I will certainly get you several cups of coffee."

I hoped he wouldn't see that as some kind of insinuation.

He smiled and said that he would get straight on it and that I had nothing to worry about.

We parted ways, but I watched him on occasion, working away, scrubbing the paint down with a large sponge and gently spraying something.

I wanted to grab a few moments to brush my hair properly and throw some more socially acceptable clothes on. It was easy to find the time, as he seemed occupied in the work.

The reflection in my mirror was pleasing now. At least I could hold some confidence about myself.

I walked out with a couple of cups of coffee, when I could see him stop to wipe his brow.

We conversed over not speaking in all the time we have been neighbours. It was nice to come together in communication over aiding a neighbour. He told me of his how his family came to the country with a mere few pennies and opened a small, Italian restaurant. Needless to say (given the size of his house), it did extremely well and expanded in size and locations. I was impressed to hear his story.

During our long conversation over coffee, the sun shone brightly and added to the enjoyment of one another's company. He mentioned his wife and children, which comforted me. I didn't need to give excuses to keep neighbourhood relationships clean!

Before we knew it, the car looked as good as new and sat nicely in the comfort of the garage.

I told Patrick that I owed him a favour, perhaps in the shape of cooking English food for him and his family.

As the evening came in, I worried about who had messed the car up with such messages. I had the odd camera about the house and decided to set some of the locations up to benefit a full look-out over the external parts.

I know we had a crazy night of fun, but there was no need for criminal damage or stalking behaviours. My nerves grew as the dark came in, but I gave myself as many comforting thoughts as I possibly could.

Chapter Three

I woke the next day, recalling some crazy dreams. It was nice to realise I had a good night's sleep. The bed was so comfortable and my head was feeling nice and clear.

I got up relatively quickly and went through camera footage to check for any unusual occurrences. Everything seemed clear, so I felt fairly relaxed and grew ready for the day.

I wasn't sure what the day held and I knew I had-to invent my entertainment or plans to make it worthwhile. My level of desiring fun was dropping, as if I had already conquered a large chunk of my desires. I referred to my list to see if anything stood out. The next task could possibly be to learn to surf! The weather looked good and the morning was still young.

I decided to ignore any calls or messages today and head out in the car to the nearest beach. It took a couple of hours to reach one of my favourite childhood locations. The sea was frighteningly vast. It had been such a long time since visiting this beach. I reached down to feel for my purse, knowing I would need to spend some money.

Walking along the beach front, I found some surf boards for sale. I asked a handsome hippy about the different types of boards. He suggested one, but advised it would be best to have some training initially. I told him that I would learn using videos, which made him chuckle. He told me to get some wax and showed me how to wax the board before trying. He was obviously concerned, as he also showed me how to carry the surfboard comfortably. I appreciated his advice, but he clearly told me to be extremely careful.

His reaction didn't bother me, so I bought the board and the wax with the intention of having some fun!

Now, after comfortably sitting on my towel, watching some training videos on my phone, I realised I was meant to have some company just in case I got into any kind of situation. I noticed I was alone in my section of the beach. It didn't dissuade me though. I decided to study the first video over and over again, to ensure I knew what to do. It wasn't important to me what others thought, as I stood up, practicing jumping up in a space of sand which represented the board for now. I was aware that I was flopping around in my bikini, but it certainly wasn't to gain attention. There were no viewers as far as I could see.

The video I was following, gave instruction to practice on sand initially before jumping onto the board. I did about two hours' worth of jumping up on the sand and my legs were starting to burn! I decided to stop for a while and eat some sandwiches I had prepared before leaving the house.

I looked up to view the beautiful ocean, with the turquoise colours blending into deeper and lighter blues. The sky was glorious. There were no clouds in the sky. I picked the best day to be here.

After the lunch rest and observation time, I stood to test my skills on the board. I managed to keep the same action pretty much, so decided to have a little body boarding in the sea. It was really warm, so it would be fun anyway. I first waxed the board as instructed, which took longer than I initially planned. Eventually I managed to get myself together enough to enjoy the fresh waters on my toes. I walked in to waist height as they instruct to do on the video.

I firstly started with the body boarding and enjoyed the feeling of riding on top of the sea. It felt exciting already. I timed it well after a while, to jump on top of the board, just as practiced and I was surprised to find that I actually managed to do it and stay on the board until I reached really shallow parts. Wow! It felt amazing! I wish I had tried it years ago.

The second attempt wasn't as fortunate, as I fell off in the early part of the jumping on. When I resurfaced and stood, I didn't realise my bikini top had slipped to the side, announcing my breasts. I looked up to see no-one directly ahead, but that someone was filming me from the side, slightly in the distance. I couldn't believe it! How cheeky.

I signalled them with my hand to stop filming, while I did my best to re-attach my material in the right places. I didn't even notice that this particular man was in range.

It didn't faze me though, as I went back out to waist height in the water. I did some body-boarding again just to discourage any onlookers for a while – make them think I am too boring to even look at.

Thankfully, the chap had moved on. He probably feared me coming out to have a word, since I was occasionally glancing over to check on his actions.

After some body-boarding, occasional jumping on and riding, my legs grew tired pretty quickly. I realised this was great exercise and desired a life near the beach. This "fun" thing was really changing my perspective on life.

I went back up onto the sand and had a lie down on my towel to rest for a while. As I began to dose slightly, I noticed a dark shadow cover my face. I opened my eyes to see a young man of about twenty-something. With shock I just managed,

"What? ..."

"I'm so sorry to give you a fright," his little voice spoke out with slight nerves. "I just wanted to let you know that there's a bloke sharing a video of you falling out of your bikini. He just showed me when we walked past each other."

"What? I knew it! Is he some kind of psycho?" was all I could manage.

I rose to my haunches and thanked the young man for the information, even though I guessed he was *that* strange.

The young man left and continued on with what looked like a long walk.

At this point I didn't want some idiot to ruin my feelings of having fun in any which way I chose, but it also made me wonder if this was the kind of repercussion that comes with living life to the full... The occasional twit to annoy you!

I decided to ignore the situation. My reasoning was that if people enjoyed looking at my breasts, then I should be happy for them. I had enough confidence in my body to flaunt it, although wouldn't do this kind of thing deliberately.

I decided not to think any more of the silly behaviour. I looked down to notice my skin turning quite a shade of pink, so grabbed my clothes and slipped them on quickly. I gazed at the sea a little more before deciding to head back to the car.

It wasn't until I reached the car, that I realised I hadn't considered the transportation of the surf board. Thankfully it wasn't the largest long-board style, so I was able to force it in with the lowering of the passenger seat. I laughed at my lack of planning. Perhaps I wasn't as intelligent as I've been led to believe. This made me laugh even more.

I also chuckled at the fact that I was exposed on video twice in a short space of time!

The drive home was filled with loud music and liberal speed on the pedal. The roads were relatively quiet and enjoyably long. I felt fantastic. Feeling a bit of speed and singing along to some fun sounds gave me excitement. I felt like I was breaking all the rules, with the loud music and racing car. Who the hell makes the rules anyway? If it feels good, I'm going to do it!

I decided I needed more times like these. The feeling was of freedom and madness. It was good getting to know myself.
As I drove, my phone rang very loudly on the hands-free. I looked down to notice Jack was trying to call. Guilt grew with the realisation I had left the poor man hanging in suspension. A conversation wouldn't do me any harm right now. I answered the call and we spoke for about half an hour, finalising on our next meet-up. We decided to meet up the next day. I thought he was worth pursuing, with the hope that he wasn't just looking for one thing.
Stupidly, this played on my mind for a few moments. After the call, I threw the music back on. The drive was almost over and I needed to think about the fun elements of the day.

All of a sudden, the car made a chugging noise and I felt it come to a halt! I couldn't believe it! My first thought was an arrogant one, such as "how can such a great car fail on one simple trip to the beach?"
As I pulled over to the nearest gap on the side of the road, I looked down at the dash and realised I had stupidly run out of fuel! This was not part of the plan! Again, maybe I wasn't as intelligent as I was led to believe! Anger of my second mistake of the day filled me intensely. I decided after a few moments that anger wouldn't do me any good and that a plan of rectification was the only useful answer. Thankfully, I was registered with a recovery service, but I

also wanted to check for a local fuel station, since I knew I had a Jerrycan in the boot that I could fill. I checked on my phone (grateful for this service) and found that I could reach a fuel station if I was willing to walk two miles down a stretch of road that didn't appear to have any side pavement.

There was plenty of battery juice on my phone, so I decided that a good walk wouldn't do any harm. I grabbed the can from the boot and began to walk.

Most of the way there I cursed myself, calling myself a plonker under my breath. I continually reminded myself of anger being of no use to me. What a battle with myself. The good thing is that walking was good for release. I picked the pace up and noticed a petrol garage in the distance, looking very small. It was like seeing a mirage in the desert, just hoping it was real! I realised how spoilt I was if this was a dramatic affair. Many people experience a heck of a lot worse.

Come on, this is all part of the adventure.

As the odd car drove past, I noticed some confused looks. I suppose it wasn't the every-day scene – a lady walking along a dangerous road with a Jerrycan! It was fun just to smile and see their expressions.

One car decided to slow down and put their hazard lights on.

A man's head reached through the passenger window.

"Do you need a lift love? You run out of fuel?"

At first I felt a bit nervous about the random car pulling up beside me.

"Oh, I'm okay. My car isn't too far away. I haven't had far to walk really. It will do me good."

The man seemed "put out" by my rejection of help. That was going by his expression, but his words confirmed it.

"Screw you then bitch!"

In the same second, the car screeched off into the distance, appearing to do a sharp handbrake turn, then raced back towards me! I felt as if my heart was about to hit my shoes and explode! Expecting them to attack me, or rob me, I jumped over a small hedge at the side of the road and ran into the field! I felt for my phone, which sat in my pocket, but just wanted to monitor their driving actions first. For the meantime I decided the best course of action was to keep running as fast as I could, but slightly into the field, still aiming for the fuel station. I wondered how close I was getting. It's so strange how so many thoughts enter the mind so swiftly, yet everything seems to be in slow motion when the adrenaline kicks in!

The car raced straight past me I noticed. It didn't stop or attempt to chase me. Thank goodness! I decided to keep running however, taking the straightest route I possibly could. The field I was in seemed very uneven and muddy, but I managed somehow. The car engine sound was most certainly in the far distance now. I just prayed they weren't planning on another spin-around and insult. I could see that the station grew larger, but also that the field had an ending to it, so I needed to find a patch of space that didn't have a large bush to jump over.

As I was moving back to the edge of the field, I was ready to jump over the lowest growth area. Lifting one foot, I stumbled and felt one ankle twist really badly.

"No!"

"Argh! Shit!"

I fell into the bush head-first instead. There seemed to be sharp brambles, that I felt scratch my face! Thankfully I closed my eyes during the fall, which was a natural saving grace.

I looked at my situation, figuring out I could still hobble painfully, noticing I was only approximately two hundred meters away from the station. I could do it quite easily.

Finally, I reached the fuel station and walked directly over to a fuel pump. I filled the can pretty quickly, wondering how much fuel these things could hold. It didn't matter however, knowing that a little would at least get me home. I wasn't too far away. The next thought I didn't contemplate was the weight of the can for the walk back. Again, I looked for a positive in my mind and decided it would be great exercise.

I walked into the shop and noticed some drinks of water and bars of chocolate.

Well, perhaps I could walk some chocolate off!

Arriving at the cash register, I noticed the observant eyes of the lady. Perhaps I did look a little dishevelled, but at this point I didn't care. I had the money, so handed it over with gratitude for the items. The lady stopped me before I walked away, with a caring question.

"Are you going to be okay with that can? Maybe I could call a taxi for you."

I was happy to hear a kind and thoughtful set of words.

"Oh, I'm sure I'll be okay thanks. I'm only a couple of miles back."

The lady frowned.

"Ah no, this isn't right. Let me see if my colleague can drop you back to your car."

"Oh no! This isn't part of your service. It's not your fault I was stupid enough to run out of fuel! If you do that for everyone you'd need to charge for an extra service."

I couldn't believe I was turning down a safe and comfortable journey back to my car.

Thankfully the lady wasn't having any of my determined thoughts.

"No, please wait here. It is certainly worth asking my colleague first before you wonder off. Please just give me a couple of minutes."

The lady wondered off into a little side room where I heard some mumbling. She came out to give some very comforting words.

"My colleague said that if you wait here for just five minutes, he can give you a lift back to your car, especially if it's only a couple of miles away. In the meantime you can clean yourself up in our public toilets over there if you like?"

She pointed to a door in the corner of the small shop.

I smiled and gave into her offer, almost feeling a moment of tearfulness. The lady obviously noticed my feelings, giving me some further encouragement to use the room.

"Go on, go and freshen yourself up."

I could feel myself smiling broader as I placed my items down near her desk.

The toilets were surprisingly bright, with three toilet cubicles. I caught sight of myself in the mirror and had a bit of a shock! Deep scratches filled my head and cheeks! One looked particularly bad, with broken skin and a slight bleed! No wonder the lady took pity on me! I couldn't believe it! I washed my face down with some lovely warm water, stinging the skin badly, making me cringe.
I looked back up to see the red marks looking so liberal and my hair appearing wiry. My fingers were able to tidy the hair up pretty well thankfully.
I looked in the mirror for quite a moment, wondering how long it would take for the scratches to heal. After that, I suddenly panicked at the thought of meeting up with Jack tomorrow!
Ah jeepers!

I plucked up the courage to head back into the shop area, feeling a little less confident, now knowing how crazy I must look!
The lady behind the till was quite busy at this point, so I was grateful for the distraction.
There was a time of silence in the shop, so I swiftly wanted to explain why I looked the way I did. The lady thankfully listened between her customers.
"I tripped while trying to jump over a bush, but ended up in it face first! I twisted my darn ankle in the process."
I could see the lady trying to hold back a chuckle.
"Ah gosh, that's not good! I did wonder what happened. I thought you'd been in some kind of cat fight."
I noticed her smiling throughout her sentence.

"Well, I nearly had a cat fight with two men. They offered me a lift, but were rude arseholes. I'm glad I didn't accept their offer like a fool. They behaved aggressively, hence me running into a field to get away from them."

The smile on the assistant's face dropped instantly as I explained.

"I think I should call the police! Don't you? What kind of aggression did they show?"

I realised how this lady's mind was thinking more logically than mine at this point.

"You know, they didn't do any harm in the end. Maybe they were just playing some kind of childish prank."

I wasn't sure if this was a soft outlook.

"Well, it's up to you, but that isn't normal behaviour, even if it's just for their intelligence. Did you get their number plate or anything?"

I realise how stupid I had been yet again.

"I only have a description of the one man's face and make and model of the car."

Maybe my other observations would make up for things.

Just as we were conversing and considering a call to the police, a scruffy looking gentleman walked from the back room carrying car keys. He was obviously the person about to give me lift.

I looked at his appearance, but then remembered mine!

This is no time for judgement!

We both toddled off down to a small car and climbed in. The man was rather quiet. I didn't know what to say other than to thank him for his kindness. He only responded with single words. I'm not sure *I* could work with someone like that!

We headed in the direction of my car and it felt a heck of a lot longer than I could measure in my mind.

In fact, I couldn't see my car on the long stretch of road for miles ahead!

The man grew a little frustrated and asked how far away I had parked. I told him it had only been a couple of miles, as I had checked on my phone maps.

After a ten minute drive, the man pulled over, into a layby.

"Hey lady, you're gonna have to tell me where yer car is."

He spoke more than one word!

I felt shocked and consumed in fear.

"I know it was definitely only two miles away. I measured it and walked it! I would have caught a taxi or called for recovery if it had been any further. Trust me, I'm not that crazy."

As I spoke, I thought about all of the scratches on my face and the fact that I had run out of fuel! I waited for a bad response about how silly I was just for not watching the fuel gauge. He didn't say anything to that formula.

"Well, I hate to say it, but maybe it's been towed away, or perhaps even... well... stolen."

I could tell he was trying to break the news gently. He looked over at me with a worried expression, as if he was expecting a full load of tears. Instead I sat in silence, wondering what to do. It suddenly hit me.

"The men!"

"Sorry, what?"

"The men!"

The man beside me didn't have a clue what I was referring to.

"Well, two men asked me if I wanted a lift, but I declined. They drove up the road shouting crap, then spun the car around and went back in the opposite direction very aggressively."

"So, these men... you think... stole your car?"

He caught on quickly.

"Yes. Oh shit. I do need to call the cops."

The man looked saddened for me.

"Well, I guess you do. Let's give you a ride back to the shop."

I smiled with gratitude for this man's exceptional kindness.

"Thank you so much. I'm sorry to have wasted your time."

He looked relaxed and gave a responsive grin.

I managed to call the police as soon as we were back. I stood at the back of the shop, as that was where I was told there would be some privacy. The Jerrycan sat on the floor next to me, along with my water bottle. I decided to eat chocolate for comfort in the end. In fact I went back into the shop to buy some more. It wasn't long before I had eaten four regular chocolate bars. At the end of the day, I needed it!

The police didn't seem surprised at my report and gave me an incident number in order to claim from my insurers. The good thing would be that I could potentially buy another great car with the insurance money. The bad thing was the inconvenience!

Much to my surprise, the gentleman from the shop offered me a lift home! I had a chance to stare at his features when talking to one another about it. He had long, straggly hair with long side burns hiding in there. I noticed he was able to string decent sentences together once he dropped his frustration act. I had the impression his workload dragged his mood down. He had an unusual accent, but a strong intelligence behind his deep brown eyes. It wasn't until we climbed back into his car that we exchanged names officially. His character certainly matched his name, "Andy".

Eventually we were already headed home and my stress levels had reduced considerably.

Patrick was working on his front garden at the time we pulled up outside of my home. I observed his occasional stare, watching his attempt to put his imaginative story of my events together. Here I was, arriving in a stranger's car, handing him money and thanking him abundantly.

Patrick was now following me with his eyes as I slowly climbed up my driveway with my Jerrycan of petrol, with scratches all over my face.
I should have been driving up to the front door, taking the newly purchased surfboard out of the car!
I could tell Patrick wanted to ask questions so desperately, but I just walked up to my front door and said "hello".

A good shower made me feel wonderful again. I looked in the mirror to see a pink face with fading scratch marks. I had certainly caught plenty of sun too.

With time to sit and relax, I contemplated the series of events over the last few days. It did seem that aiming to have fun, ran into some really sticky points. Strangely I was seeing everything with great humour.
I just wanted the two thieves to get caught. Despite that, I had a vision of going through some car brochures and picking something even better. I would be in a winning situation with all of this somehow.

I decided the evening would involve watching rubbish television with a big glass of wine.

It was fair to say that it would be okay to inspect my phone for messages or missed calls. I noticed that Jason was keen to meet up again. Jack was asking how I was, which scored some points in my mind. Kerry and Claire were saying that things were beginning to blow over at home already after the video madness, much to my relief! It was nice to hear from people. I began to miss mixing with the people I usually associated with. It was surprising for me to actually think that I was *also* missing work! Maybe just a few more days and I'll see if I can creep back in.

After quite a large glass of wine, I decided to head for bed.
It was early, but it certainly didn't matter.

I don't know if I confused my body by going to bed too early, but I did notice I was tossing and turning quite a lot with restlessness. The sleep was deep when I actually slept, but there was a lot of movement that's for sure.

I dropped into a weird dream at one point. It seemed so real though! It felt as if a doctor was coming into my room to look at my arm then began to administer an injection. As soon as the injection was about to pierce the skin, I woke with a start! The dream seemed so real that I checked around the room and swear I felt a draft of movement at the same time. From the corner of my eye I noted a grey swirl of movement in the air, perhaps the shape of a foot disappearing. It was so strange! The only way I could describe it was as if someone had moved so fast that the human eye couldn't quite capture them. There was the glimpse of the grey smear mixed with the final image of the foot, moving out of view, yet it all blended together. I still couldn't quite explain what I had seen. All I could do was put it down to the *dream* and my imagination continuing on. The last time I experienced anything like that was when I was a kid. I remember dreaming of skulls floating around the room. I thought I was awake, but I suddenly woke up staring at the same spot, with faded skulls still in view. It was frightening at the time, but all of it went in the brain box of "dreams" and imagination.

After the strange and unsettled night, I woke to find my left arm a
bit tender.

That bloody doctor!

I was blaming the doctor in my dream for this!

I put it down to sleeping peculiarly.

There was no evidential cause otherwise.

I went about my morning as I usually did, grabbing my breakfast
and throwing myself together with clothes and a bit of make-up.
The scratches on my face looked a heck of a lot better! I noticed
just one fine line of red left, going from the top of my forehead all
of the way down over the top of my nose and falling slightly onto
my cheek. It didn't look great, but it was almost perfect after the
way I appeared yesterday!

I was due to see Jack later today, but I felt a bit apprehensive about
it. This was only because I wasn't in the mood for madness today
after yesterday's events. Perhaps seeing him would lift me back up
to the desire of fun! I talked myself into it. We weren't meeting
until a bit later, so I had time to put my feet up and watch some
silly videos online. I grew too comfortable to move after a while,
but knew it would be good for me to get up and head out.

Jack was waiting for me in a coffee shop not too far from my place. It was a different scene and the thought of a hot drink and cake really appealed to me. We found each other and obtained the perfect drink and cake combination for each of us. It was already a heavenly scene for me - tantalising the taste buds!

Jack looked good. He was wearing a tee-shirt that clung to his body shape. His chest was nicely shaped and his abs lovely and flat. I wasn't materialistic in any way, but it was a nice view for me. His hair was sharp and not over-gelled. He was someone I could certainly stare at for a while. It seemed a conversation point.

"So, do you like the way I dressed for you today?" He asked with a gentle tone.

Shit, don't say it. It ruins the whole "He made no effort assumption".

I wish he hadn't said that as if looking for a compliment.

"Oh, yes, I certainly do."

"Well, come on in here." He pulled my chair closer to him and started to kiss me with some heavy enthusiasm.

I must've given a weaker level of interest, given his pause.

"Hey, what's up?"

I didn't get the chance to explain the scratch on my face and nor did he even ask!

"Well, I had a bit of a strange day yesterday. I know we've exchanged messages to update each other with events, but I ended up injuring an ankle and scratching my face in a prickly bush! I'm in a bit of a recovery mood I'm afraid to say."

He moved back with his head and studied my face.

"Well heck! I didn't even notice your scratch! I didn't even notice a limp! You must be great at covering things up!"

He recovered well from his lack of observation.

"Well, I suppose I tried my best with makeup and supportive boots."

"Hey, we could have postponed this if you weren't in the mood to meet up."

He finally showed a little bit of compassion. It gave me a little more confidence in the type of person he was.

"Oh, I'm mostly fine. It just means I'm repairing physically and emotionally really."

I could see his face drop, as if he was thinking his luck was out today! I couldn't help but apologise.

"Oh, I'm sorry. I don't want to dampen the mood. I still want to enjoy my time with you."

His smile reappeared and he reached in to hold the bottom of my chin, encouraging another kiss. This time he had more tenderness about him.

Maybe this guy was actually a nice guy!

We kissed for a while and then encouraged one another to enjoy the hot drink, which was now more of a warm drink. The cake we had looked delicious, so we both devoured them in good time.

After relaxing in one another's arms for a few moments, Jack suggested a gentle stroll through a large park. I agreed, since the sun was so inviting.

We stood to leave, finding ourselves feeling quite full from our treats. Perhaps a walk was a good idea!

As we were walking, I noticed my left arm started to ache again. I looked at it briefly to notice one of my veins appeared to be throbbing! It was an odd feeling and appearance. The vein looked as if it was growing and pumping harder than usual. I tried to behave normally in front of Jack despite my slight concern.

Jack was quite distracting anyway, as he started asking about my sexual experiences and if I had ever attempted a threesome! I wasn't sure if he was hoping for something, or trying to gain some history from me. Perhaps I was giving the impression of being a bit "easy". At this point I wondered if I should start slipping pieces of my real-self into conversations, just a gradual and gentle introduction, stage by stage. I still wanted the fun, but I didn't want him to think that I was an easy lay. He seemed to notice, I could tell by his body language. It was a delicate balance, so I occasionally threw some surprising flirtations into the equation. I noticed his reactions to each offering I gave. He was obviously very keen on anything sexual. I guess I had been out of this game for far too long. Anyone who could hear my thoughts would know how far behind in life I was!

We walked to a patch of comfortable looking grass, in front of the edge of a wonderful lake. Jack surprisingly grappled me in a controlled way, tackling me to the ground. At first I was shocked at the sudden move, but I went with it and ended up landing softly on the wonderful grass. He initially moved over me to give me a nice, loving kiss and then rolled over to his side to hold me with one arm, looking over onto a lake. I thought it was all sweet and romantic.

Swans were drifting over to take a look at us, most likely to see if we had any free food, making us feel guilty momentarily.

Someone in a small canoe paddled over towards us and managed to board tightly enough on land to climb out relatively comfortably. It reminded me of my surfing attempt.

The man left his canoe and paddles on the grass, after pulling it up with a struggle. He then walked off with intention. We didn't see where he was headed.

Jack suggested we borrow the canoe, since the man had disappeared for quite some time.

I was surprised at his naughty suggestion and said "no!"

The man was certainly missing for some time however, so it was a temptation. It was a large canoe, one for two!

Jack seemed to find it difficult to resist his desire.

"We could return it really quickly. I reckon he's gone off for lunch somewhere."

"No! It's theft!"

"It's only theft if we take it with the intention of keeping it. We will return it in good time, before he even notices."

"Why do you want to do it? Just ignore the canoe and focus on me!"

I grabbed my head in a gesture to kiss me some more. He complied briefly, but turned his eyes occasionally as he truly had an addiction to his idea.

"Come on!" He shouted whilst running a few steps towards the canoe.

I sat up in shock!

"We can't Jack! What if he's watching from a distance?"

"Come on! Let's take the risk!"

I couldn't believe his thoughts and actions. I surprised myself too, by standing, but cautiously viewing everything by three hundred and sixty degrees. There was literally no soul about that I could see.

"Can you swim?"

At least he was checking on our health and safety!

"I am a strong swimmer, but why do you want to do this?"

"I just want to be a bit daring and have some fun."

He looked a bit surprised on my questioning, as if it was normal to play with someone else's valuables.

I realised that perhaps I was being contradictory, when *I* was the one who wanted the fun in my life. The sudden realisation of this made me want to snap out of my caution and go for the fun aspect. I ran up to the canoe.

"Come on then!"

He smiled at my change of action and ran over to aid me into the canoe.

We both managed to get in without too much issue and pushed off into the large lake with one of the paddles.

Before we knew it, we were floating amongst the swans and occasional duck! I would look around occasionally, checking for the man's return. My watch showed that we had been in the canoe, floating around for over an hour already, with no sign of the man's return. The sun was gorgeous and the water was so sparkly, but I couldn't fully relax knowing we may get called over by the police if we weren't careful. I then saw a boring image of myself in my mind and snapped out of the silly fearfulness, deciding to relax. Just as my psychological barriers went down, I spotted a male figure similar to the image I had remembered. I noticed him walking towards the original spot of his canoe!

"Jack! Jack! The man is coming back!" I didn't mean to rhyme! He spun to see the figure walking nearer in a casual manner, holding onto a bag of something.

"Shit!"

Jack was genuinely panicking and paddling in a disorderly fashion, trying to gain control of the direction we were headed. I noticed he was aiming to go behind some trees and shrubs. We pulled between some trees as predicted. Jack pulled me out gently once we managed to reach the shallow ground. We were now both on foot, with the canoe tucked away, out of sight. It was hard to pretend to walk normally without any guilt, but we just about managed it.

I looked back to see the man obsessively hunting around for his asset. He reached into his bag and grabbed what looked like a baton!   I encouraged Jack to speed up and rush out of sight. It was quite hard for me however, as I was wearing some uncomfortable shoes. I stumbled and fell, just as the ones do in the annoying horror films that keep you on the edge of your seat. As I fell, I looked up to see the man running towards us with what did seem to be his weapon!

"Jack!" I shouted with a whisper as he literally dragged me to my feet.

"We are showing guilt!" Jack whispered in return. "Just walk normally."

I looked back to see the man gaining on us.

"No! He knows. I think I've given it away with my behaviour."

"Argh! Well, change your behaviour."

I didn't know how to!

"Jack, he's gaining on us and he has some kind of bat, or baton.

"He can't harm us, or prove that we've done anything. Just walk normally."

"What if he caught sight of us? What if he put two and two together? We're the obvious culprits."

"Jenny! Calm down and act normal."

I noticed the man really gaining distance, perhaps only two hundred meters away now. I looked forward and tripped again! I couldn't believe how stupid I was being. Jack couldn't believe it either.

"What the hell? Remind me not to use you as my getaway!"

At the time I couldn't see the funny side of anything and just remained on the floor. I told Jack to get down on the ground with me.

"Join me on the floor." I whispered loudly.

"What?"

"Just join me and get on top of me. Pretend you want some passion right now."

He complied and dropped down to join me on the floor.

We kissed and I had a sneaky eye on the approaching man. He looked as if he dropped from an angry emotion to a confused one. I grabbed Jack and pulled him closer. We were pretending to get into a good fondling session. I closed my eyes tight, feeling the shadow of the man now over us.

"Excuse me Sir and Ma'am, have you seen my boat?"

All of a sudden I was able to use an innocent, acting face, now that I was stuck in the moment.

"Oh, why would I see anyone's boat? Unless it was in an unusual place, like on the grass up here."

I notice the man looked a bit confused.

"Oh I am sorry dear. I have lost my boat you see. I left it in a certain place and just went off to get some gear. Now it's missing."

I thought I was playing my role really well.

"Oh, did you want us to come to help you find it?"

The man looked thoughtful.

"Ah, not just yet, I am sure it must have just drifted up the lake perhaps."

"Okay then." I returned to face our romantic acting.

I could tell he felt awkward and walked away stage by stage.

Jack started whispering but I couldn't quite hear him. I checked on the man's direction and knew we could now speak liberally.

"He's gone now."

Jack didn't want to move however.

"I can't really move at the moment."

I noticed Jack was very excited.

"Well, we can't do it here!"

"I think we should. It would really frighten everyone away."

"Jack, we're doubling our chances of getting arrested."

He realised the truth and looked about, before trying to tuck everything back down!

A couple were innocently walking up the path beside the lake, not too far away from us.

"We need to keep moving."

Jack pulled himself up from the ground and lifted me kindly from my hands.

We walked briskly back to the car park of the coffee shop.

During the walk, I had time to explain my events for having had my car stolen. He offered me a lift in his van back to mine. I knew his obvious hopes, but I did fancy a lift back.

We arrived back at mine in no time and had a really good snog in the van. I knew Jack was trying to entice me for an invite in, but I didn't want to encourage it. It didn't feel like the right time to have him in my home. The only error would be him knowing where I lived!

We said our goodbyes and I could tell he was slightly disappointed. As I banged the van door shut, I turned to see that the neighbour, Patrick, was standing in the garden, pruning some of his rose bushes back. I couldn't believe he would be witnessing another man dropping me off at my home. I spoke to him as I walked up the drive.

"Hello Patrick."

"Jenny... Hi."

It was obvious he was observing my actions. I did recall the day he had aided in the cleaning of my car. The words "Slut" might have been making sense to his judgement right now!

I didn't feel like giving an explanation however, since everything was innocent. Well, reasonably innocent!

The house was cool inside and the light was nice and bright. I felt positive and knew that my fun levels were certainly increasing, but it was also elevating a certain amount of risk. It didn't seem to matter though, as I always managed to escape the seemingly 'dangerous' moments.

It heightened my bravery and I was almost daring myself to take part in more challenging versions of fun! At this stage I couldn't see myself returning to work. I was going to make the most of every minute of this free time now. I didn't even know what day it was! It was affecting me in a wonderful way at this moment in time.

I enjoyed yet another evening of rubbish television and a large glass of wine. It was wonderful to just have some time to myself.

That night my arm was really bugging me. I wasn't sure what I had done to it. In the middle of the night I was forced to get up and take a pain killer. I couldn't believe it. It better not ruin my chances of fun!

The next morning I rose feeling surprisingly bright and comfortable, so I relaxed knowing all was okay.

Breakfast involved looking at my free, local paper, just randomly. In there I found an advertisement for Go Karting.
Anyone looking down on me would be saying, "Oh here we go."
I wasn't sure if it was for me, but then I felt like some kind of water sport again. The weather was fine and my body was feeling

like some exercise. The only missing feature to my freedom was my car! I was expecting to have a courtesy car delivered at some point, so I decided to chase it up.

Thankfully they were happy to deliver the temporary car at eleven o'clock. Wow! I can plan some fun. Perhaps I could see if Jason was free at all. Ooh!

After some messages were sent backwards and forwards, Jason was able to escape work for the rest of the day to join me. I challenged him to any water sport of his choice. We decided to have a go at water skiing at some local water parks. Neither of us had ever tried it, so it was worth a unique attempt.

I agreed to meet him at the venue to avoid another date knowing my home location.

My courtesy car arrived early, so I was able to play around with all of the new buttons in good time for familiarity. I felt so fortunate to have arranged the hire car facility on my insurance! I wasn't sure how long I could borrow it for, but I wasn't going to hang around with purchasing a new one just as soon as my money was due.

This was a sporty red convertible, which was a good image! Whilst out playing with this new toy, I felt Patrick's eyes on me from one of his windows. I didn't think about how this might have looked. He had made such an effort to help clean my previous one up. Perhaps I would gain chance to explain all of my recent actions to him one day soon!

I drove off to meet up with Jason at the venue. He was looking extremely fit and ready for sporting action, even better than our ice skating event! Wow!

We stopped for a drink in the provided café to catch up first. He admitted to feeling a bit nervous about this new challenge. We exchanged thoughts, not entirely knowing what we had signed up for! We were, however very fortunate to be able to book an event with such short notice. I was quite excited to share something different with a hunk by my side!

We changed into provided wet gear in the separate changing rooms, once we completed our booking-in stage.
Jason looked amazingly suited to the wetsuit and life jacket! He also seemed to acquire some footwear for water. I wasn't offered that, but hoped my feet were safe! I was hoping we could have stripped down to our swimming costumes, but the organisers were advising against it on our first experience. It was also a little bit fresh in the air that day, so I expected some cold water. Upon those thoughts, it was certainly "fair enough" on the wet gear!

Our instructor treated us as if we were an old couple. I enjoyed that so chose not to correct him. Jason seemed to be comfortable with it too. We smiled knowingly at one another every now and then.

We managed to take to the skis fairly quickly and only fell off when we appeared to grow tired each time.

The vein in my arm seemed to throb again. I really didn't understand it. Perhaps I should definitely get it seen to after this fun event. I think I hid my occasional concern quite well though! Each time I looked at my arm, the vein did visually appear to throb! It seemed to expand and then contract to the normal size. It was so strange! I know that our veins appear a blueish colour when we look at them, but it appeared to be more of a green colour when it expanded! I was secretly quite frightened by it.

I could see that Jason was enjoying himself and occasionally holding on to the handles with one hand, trying to build his confidence. I was keen to focus hard and stick to holding on tight! It was great fun!

Jason looked over at a time I stumbled and fell into the water. As I fell, I gained a great cramp in my arm and could barely move. I kept myself under the water to contain my painful expression. The water seemed pretty clear, so I took a sneak peek at my arm. The vein expanded to almost the same size as my forearm! What the heck was happening to me? Within the few seconds I was under water, the vein split in the middle and opened up to what seemed to be a valve! It looked as if it was breathing. I went into some kind of shock and felt myself disappearing into blackness.

I found myself coughing and choking on the air itself all of a sudden. My eyes opened to a bright sky and two faces hovering over me.

"There you are!" I noticed the instructor's face hovering over me and Jason kneeling on the opposite side.

I looked around to see that I was on some kind of paving, lying on my back. Everything was a little confusing, as one second I was under water, looking at my strange arm thing, and the next I was relaxing on the ground, looking at two handsome faces.

"What happened?" My voice seemed a bit croaky.

The instructor looked at me with concern.

"I think you fainted under water. I'm not sure, so we have an ambulance coming to check on you."

I sat up and felt perfectly fine.

"I think you're right. I was shocked by something and just seemed to black out."

"Yes. You were under water for a few seconds, so Jason went in to get you, but I think we grabbed you in good time. You were still breathing fine and your pulse was still perfect."

I was impressed with myself.

"I don't think I need an ambulance. I think I just frightened myself." I looked down at my arm to see that it was perfectly normal again!

"Ah well, let's just be on the safe side. They can at least confirm your vitals."

"Argh, okay."

Jason smiled at my reluctance. He looked amazing and he was proving his worth in this situation. I must've looked a right state!

The instructor walked off to seemingly go and draw any due ambulance in. Jason looked at me again with a smile.

"You frightened me. You were completely out of it."

"Ah, I'm so sorry! You must think I'm very strange."

He frowned in disgust almost!

"Jenny, you are so hot, even when you're unconscious!"

I laughed with hope that he was being honest. Perhaps another couple of dates would test his words.

Before we knew it, a couple of ambulance crew members checked me over and said I was perfectly fine. They said that my heart seemed very strong. I admit that their confirmation made me feel more courage about myself. I decided to ask them about my arm. It just seemed the right thing to do while they had made a visit. It didn't appear to be odd in any way to them, so I couldn't explain my experience. I wasn't brave enough to tell them *exactly* what had happened, just that it was painful! They may encourage some "psych ward!" I knew it wasn't my imagination, but nobody would believe such a thing surely!

Jason suggested we call the rest of the challenge off and head back over for some drinks and sugary items in the café. I had no reluctance to that!

We sat in the café, enjoying a great conversation for hours! It didn't matter if we stopped the skiing, as the date was fantastic, despite the strange events. I wondered if I was imagining the arm thing, or even if I had eaten something that my mind didn't like! I was thinking of all sorts of excuses, trying to make sense of it. Our conversation flowed despite my private analysing.

The thing I really enjoyed about Jason deep down, was the fact that he wasn't just after my body. Perhaps he was and just biding his time, but he didn't rush for it! It impressed me.

It seemed a shame that Jason didn't have the situation of being able to drop me off at home. That kind of finalisation to a date is lovely. It was at my control however. I decided on it for various reasons. One of the reasons being the risk of random visits clashing when dating more than one man!
At the end of the date however, we did share a nice kiss next to my borrowed car! He said he liked the car too, so I didn't admit to it not being mine. I enjoyed a bit of flattery at the moment, although the thought did hit me that I may need to explain another car soon. Ah well! That's assuming I get to see Jason again. I hoped we had enough excitement between us to enjoy further dates.
The problem I would find is splitting the differences between Jason and Jack! They were both great men I never expected to even come in contact with. One I've rushed things a little with, but don't have any regrets. The other I've had some honest experiences with. Hmm, further dates required!
I chuckled to myself.

Jason and I said our goodbyes for now.

At home it was tricky for me to relax about the arm situation. I kept staring at my vein, wondering why it wasn't always throbbing. A mind set was needed to remain calm. It didn't happen again since the skiing incident, so I decided to simply let it all go.

Chapter Four

I decided it was healthy to have some girl-time. Although it was part of my usually-boring routine, I decided it would be healthy to get back to the Yoga. I met up with Karen beforehand to have a nice meal and chat, with the plan to go to our class shortly after. She listened to my date dilemmas after finally admitting I was seeing the *two* men! I listened to her reminiscing of our drunken night. We certainly had some chuckles. Karen was happy to hear that I was actually living my life, although she criticised the fact that it was a little late! I disagreed mildly, knowing that I still had time to make up for things. I was certainly having a blast!

The Yoga class felt pretty flat after all of the mad things I was conquering daily. I knew it was good for me though, so I shook the negative thinking away. It was good to see my friends together in one group. They all commented on how refreshed I seemed. I felt stronger than usual and more vibrant in every sense. It was nicely odd! I wasn't going to complain however. The observation was great! I could lift my bodyweight without any effort at all. Perhaps the break from the class allowed some healing in some shape or form. A replenishment of the muscle cells maybe. I did check my body over, but didn't see any difference in any shape. My arm was behaving itself too.
There was only one odd observation during my movements and that was that my toes seemed to spread further to give more balance in movement. They did seem to spread further than I

remembered them spreading before, but I put it down to never really paying attention to how they would normally behave.

When I arrived home, I felt wonderfully refreshed and balanced. It wasn't late, but I fancied a nice softening bath to soak in. Water was something I couldn't seem to get enough of lately!

I climbed into the bath, with the intention to completely relax. It was normal for me to have the odd candle on the edges of the bathtub, so I added the feature of lighting them all up. I was also making habit of having a large glass of wine in the evenings, so I ensured I had a little table by the side for the glass. This was bliss! There was a slight interruption of things when I felt my arm begin to throb again! I couldn't believe it! Panic began to set in, as I cautiously lifted my arm from the bubbles to take a look. Once again, a slit began to form in the place of the vein area!
No! This cannot be happening!
I didn't know who I could see about such an unusual event. At my age, I had enough logic to know that this wasn't normal! I was checked over by Paramedics, who confirmed I was perfectly healthy.
I made a brave effort to stare at my arm and figure out what was happening. It looked like a large, green, rubbery type of gill. It didn't seem real. I plucked up the courage to touch it and it felt slimy!
Eeeuw!!
The bath comforts were no longer noticeable. I sat up straight, touching, prodding and pulling this strange flappy thing about! A

'human-fish gill' was the only description I could allow my mind to have. I placed it under the bubbles of the bath and pulled it back up out of the water, to notice no difference. If it was a gill, then I wanted to test its ability! This was going to be a risk, but I decided to roll onto my front and allow myself to head completely under the water. Whilst under, I observed the arm and it did appear to open and close just like a fish gill! I pushed up, to gasp for air with panic! This couldn't be real!

Calming breaths... Yoga breaths!

This couldn't be real!

I decided to look again, but this time hold myself under the water for a moment longer.

It was still nerve-wracking, but I needed to face this and calculate what was going on. The same thing occurred, but this time I wondered how long I could stay under water without breathing. It was shocking to find that I didn't seem to need to breathe at all! I panicked about my usual breathing methods. Had I become an amphibian? How could this be possible? Who could I talk to about this?

I climbed from the bath tub and rolled onto the floor. For some reason I decided to crawl back into my bedroom. The thought of the dream of the doctor came flooding back to me.

What if a doctor really did come in and put something into my arm? Have I got any camera footage? Is this why I really fancy water sports so much lately? Why me? Why am I a weird one?

I think I went a little crazy after this. I moved to view my camera screens and went through all of the footage with speed and intensity. All footage went back to the night of the dream, yet nothing untoward had occurred. Nothing out of the ordinary!

My arm returned to normal, thankfully, once I dried myself off. I realised then that the obvious cause was water! So the plan should perhaps be to avoid water! I was worried for every bath or shower of the future!

I walked around in just a pair of knickers, trying to work out any possible weakness for point of entry into my house! My windows and doors were always sealed tight and securely. I have always been super security conscious. I just couldn't explain any of it! I was starting to connect it to the wine I was drinking. Perhaps it was creating imaginative scenes before my eyes.
I disagreed with that thought instantly! It didn't hurt to have some *more* wine either! I needed to drown myself into a drunken state, just this once!

I woke to a calm start, sprawled diagonally across my bed, still in the same underpants and a drinking glass just out of arm's reach. The sun was blasting in through the windows that I hadn't tucked away with curtains for the night. It didn't bother me however and I was just simply grateful that I had slept so well.

I wasn't sure how to take this new version of my life, but I knew I still needed to face everything, each day at a time.

The puzzle needed unravelling.

I got up and slowly paced to my cupboard, catching sight of myself in a mirror. My hair was upside down and inside out, but I didn't care. The hangover was barely there thankfully; just a small feeling of dehydration and discomfort, which would soon be rectified by breakfast habits. In fact, despite the small worry of what was happening to me, I actually felt extremely fit and strong. I was very tempted to go for a run!

No! I would need a shower afterwards! I can't have a shower!

I was about to become a very smelly person! Although I did wonder if a sponge-down method would avoid the arm's strange actions. At this point I was too nervous to even try. I just needed some time to let things settle in my mind for a few days. Work then popped up into my head. In some ways I wished work was occurring in order to distract me!

After breakfast and a quick wash-down in the bathroom, everything was normal enough for me to head outside for some fresh air. I still felt like heading out for a run, but I needed something else to distract me. The garden looked as if it needed some attention. It wasn't too bad, but perhaps I could get it looking more presentable. I looked down at my clothing, contemplating another change for the dirty work. Just as I did, I heard a voice interrupt my peace.

"Jenny! Jenny!"

It took a few seconds for me to recognise the little face inside the van that had just pulled up.

Oh no.

I can't face him today of *all* days. I had a feeling this would happen at some point however.

"Jack?" I played along.

"Hi! Fancy a night away from here?"

Straight to the point! No "*how are you*" or "*are you free for a while?*"

I looked at him then looked up to see if Patrick was peering through any windows.

Jack was hanging his arm out of the van window, witnessing my thoughts.

"I think you'd enjoy it, my boss has given me expense money for the evening and I have a hotel room booked."

I decided it was better to walk over to his van for a close range conversation. My face must have shown my feelings, so he explained further.

"I just thought this could be something different. There's a job near the coast and I wondered if you fancied a dinner and hotel room for the night with me; A bit of adventure."

All I could see was the risk of my gill-like arm popping out in the sea breeze! With a few seconds of thought, I remembered there were no major gill-like experiences with my last beach trip. This bit of fun could be just what I needed.

"Well, I suppose I could, if you give me chance to put a bag of bits together."

Jack's grin grew wider. I knew he just wanted to get into my pants, but perhaps with him working during the day, I could look for another surf board to play with. The thought of water was making me feel extremely excited now. It worried me, with the fact that it was more than the "normal" part of me that desired the water.

I decided to have a "fuck it" attitude about me though. This ridiculously weird thing wasn't going to stop me from having fun. Today was a new day!

I ran in to grab my toilet bag and a fresh pair of clothes, along with some beach gear and ran back to the van before Jack had time to complain. He grinned as I jumped into the passenger side.

"I didn't think you were keen on coming by the look on your face."

"Ah, it was just a surprise. I was contemplating doing my garden."

"What? I'm glad I saved you!"

Jack put the radio on and we were soon on our journey.

The journey was long enough to enjoy some conversation and singing without long awkward silences. We seemed to get on well.

We pulled up to the car park of a hotel. It looked quite nice from the outside. Walking in impressed me too! The room we were given was bright and spacious. My usual experiences were of dark and gloomy rooms. We threw our bags on the bed and played with the television remote. I looked at the food and drink menu for room service, wondering how much Jack had to spend on expenses. Such a cheeky thought!

He grabbed me and pushed me onto the bed, forcing the bags onto the floor.

"Already?"

This was my automatic word between the kissing moments.

He stopped and tilted his head back.

"We don't have to."

I pulled him in and encouraged the kisses, giving him my permission. I thought, "What the heck."

For some odd reason, his strength didn't seem very strong this time. I knew he was trying to be spontaneous and passionate, but my mind was focussed on how strong I felt. I decided I would show him some dominance, so grabbed his shoulders and threw him onto his back. He looked shocked, but on his soft landing, he grinned with interest. This was *my* moment of control.

I grabbed his belt and pulled it through the hoops, just for more drama, since I could have simply undone the buckle!

I pulled his zip down and ripped his jeans off with no effort, a bit like pulling a table cloth off a table swiftly enough to leave some ornaments in place!

He frowned slightly with my forceful actions, but slipped back to his happy grin swiftly.

I gripped his shoulders down, tightly into the mattress and took my top and bra off within seconds, re-placing my hands to keep him down. I noticed his eyes light up, with a slight worry in his smile. He tried to gently unravel the jeans I was wearing, but with his awkwardness, I helped him speed things up. It only took a few seconds for me to complete the job. I noticed a radio by the bedside and hit the "on" button. Jack didn't seem impressed by that part. The noise of the music seemed to distract him adversely. I didn't care though. This is what *I* wanted. I decided that I was in control this time.

He looked a bit nervous again, but I reached down to give him a sensual kiss. This pleased him. His eyes closed and he sank into thoughts of desire. I felt so strong, that it seemed that I was trapping my prey! Jack felt like one of my victims.

What the heck was wrong with me! Maybe this is my secret sexual desire coming out!

I got a little carried away and bounced on Jack, moving his body from one angle to another with no effort what so ever.

I closed my eyes, as my mind was controlled by my feelings, so I wasn't paying attention to my actions completely.

"Jenny! Jenny! Stop! Stop!" he shouted in dismay.

I thought he may have been getting a bit dramatic, or that perhaps he had heard someone trying our door out, but when I opened my eyes, I couldn't believe the position I was in!

He was pinned up against the wall behind the head of the bed. I had trapped him underneath my hands and feet, but this wasn't normal at all! I was almost crushing him with my body weight.

My hands and feet were like webbed feet, with some kind of super stickiness, or suction! They were literally stuck to the wall! I looked again and then looked down to see Jack looking red and sweaty in the face.

"Shit! I am so sorry! I got carried away!"

With might and intention, I managed to release my hands and feet from the wall and push myself back onto the bouncy mattress, allowing Jack to regain his balance. He stood on the bed, holding onto his neck, regaining his normal breathing.

I looked down at my hands and they retracted to the normal appearance thankfully!

"Wowsers! You need to control your strength! What kind of woman are you?" His tone was angry.

Jack was shocked and uncomfortable. I felt super powerful and invigorated however. Strangely, I didn't feel any remorse, as I was still caught up in the moment. Jack reached over to the ground and stood, collecting himself then walked over to the bathroom silently. It wasn't until then that I realised I needed to speak to him.

"Jack, I'm sorry. I got carried away."

He was obviously cleaning himself up and trying to recover.

"Carried away? Wow! Is that what '*carried away*' is?"

I felt as if I was getting a telling off by one of my parents.

"I'm sorry. I was just doing what felt natural to me, given our excitement."

He walked out of the bathroom, everything hanging out, looking really red and raw.

"Excitement ... Do you lift breeze blocks for entertainment? How does a lady get that strong?" Jack was clearly very unhappy.

"You don't like the fact that I'm strong?" I asked with concern and complete innocence.

"Jenny, do you realise you lifted my entire bodyweight and pinned me onto the wall? Do you realise you trapped me there and barely allowed me to breathe? Don't you see why I am red all over? Don't you realise your own strength?"

As he was speaking I looked down at my hands and feet, checking for the webbed appearance again. It didn't return thankfully at this point. I should have been shocked by the events too, but for some reason I wasn't!

"What the hell *was* that all about?" Jack just couldn't understand my sudden strength.

It was a strange situation, as we both just stood there looking at each other. I thought he was overreacting and he must have thought I simply didn't understand my own strength.

I looked at his parts and they really did look red! Part of me wanted to laugh, but I didn't want to aggravate the situation any further. He calmed himself and was the first to speak.

"Look, maybe we should both shower and head over to the dining area for a nice meal huh?"

I was stuck for words, since this was just as unusual for me as it was for him, except I felt good!

My only immediate concern was the shower! Strangely, I seemed so much calmer about all of the strange things occurring to me. It was almost as if this enhanced side of me - was now part of me.

Jack looked at me, waiting for a response to his suggestion.

"Oh, well, if you're sure we can enjoy each other's company after all of this?"

Jack's shoulders dropped forward. I could see that he was softening.

"Hey, I'm sorry I kicked off. You are freakishly strong, but maybe next time, you could just relax and let me do the work?" He looked a little nervous when obviously visualising another attempt.

I was so insanely calm about the whole situation. I was still me, but I was an enhanced me! My body and mind appeared to be synchronising in strength.

I was distracted by a conversation I could hear outside of the room door, so I decided to listen in. Jack was still stood in the same position, waiting for me to respond again.
I could hear people saying that they were getting annoyed with the shouting going on in our room. Jack prompted me for *some* kind of response during my distraction.

"Oh, sorry Jack, I was distracted by those people talking outside."

Jack turned to listen in, obviously having not heard anything.

I realised I must have better hearing than him. For some reason I told him what I could hear.

"Oh... They were complaining about the noise in here. Whoops! Ah well, I think perhaps you're right about a meal and you taking control next time."

Jack frowned. "Wow. You're summarising everything without a care."

With his response, I felt like an insensitive person while he was the over-sensitive one.

"Jack, please let's just try to enjoy this weekend. If we can't, then I can afford to book another room if you prefer."

He seemed shocked.

"Jenny, where is the person I met? It's like you've had a personality transplant. Come to that, perhaps even a strength enhancement. Have you taken something?"

His accusation of drug taking put me off this entire weekend idea. I wasn't sure if we should continue seeing each other, as things were getting a little icy!
It may have been a little hasty of me, but I redressed myself swiftly and picked my bag up from the floor, deciding it was best for both of us if I just left.

He was absolutely shocked, still standing there with his red bits hanging out. I knew it was the right thing to do however, as he didn't shout for me to change my mind, or to return. He didn't attempt to grab an arm as I passed him. Perhaps with fear of my reactive strength!

I realised this was for the best.

When I found the nearest road, I wasn't sure whether I wanted to stay near the coast for a while, or find some transportation home. I needed to flush the crazy sexual event from my mind.

I decided to run to the nearest train station, following the GPS on my phone. It didn't take too long and I was soon in a train cabin on my way home.

During the journey, everything suddenly hit me!

What was happening to me? Have I evolved? Or just been exposed to something? Should I be seeing a doctor?

All of these thoughts and more came flooding through me. I needed some comfort or an explanation.

On the journey, I decided to make an appointment online with my nearest general practitioner. I managed to get one sorted for the early evening, which should easily match my return with some extra time.

On my walk to the doctors, I wondered how I was going to put this to words.

"Oh, hello, I get a gill pop up on my arm when I go into water. My feet and hands can suddenly web-up and hold suction enough to pin my bodyweight onto walls!"

I laughed at the idea of all of this.

Before I knew it, I sat in the doctor's surgery, feeling unusually calm.

There was the usual question from the doctor to prompt the patient.

"So, what can I help you with today?"

I didn't know where to start!

"Well, I seem to be having some unusual occurrences."

"Do go on…"

"My body seems to be going through some changes."

I could see the doctor was assuming I was talking about hormonal changes!

"Not that kind of occurrence. I have a vein in my arm that throbs so badly, which opens up to…"

I needed to stop my sentence. The doctor looked at my arm when I was speaking and I could tell with his immediate frown that he wouldn't be able to explain what I was about to describe.

Thoughts of speaking to a really good friend might be more valuable! I knew this wasn't physically possible. Or was it? I think I just needed some emotional support. I'm not going to get it from this doctor.

"Actually, I've just realised there isn't anything you can do about it."

The doctor encouraged me to sit and continue to explain.

"Don't worry I think this is something I can handle. I'm really sorry to have wasted your time."

The doctor frowned and then instantly raised his eyebrows with acceptance.

I walked out feeling like I'd just told a doctor that he would be completely useless in this situation.

This was going to be something I needed to deal with in my own head, but to share it with someone close would at least halve any stress. It needed to be someone I could trust completely.

A friend I haven't seen for years, but known since Primary School was always someone I could turn to. We would usually catch up months ahead as if we were never away from each other.

Sue was like a second mother to me at times, but I felt that I reciprocated just as often.

I wasn't sure how I was going to explain such strange experiences however. Even a great friend may think they're doing the right thing by suggesting a therapist!

I needed to take the risk though. This couldn't be dealt with alone!

Thankfully, all that Jack witnessed was super strength. No-one as yet has seen the ridiculous arm "gill", or the webbed hands and feet that have powerful suction! How the hell do you explain that? Even to your lifetime friend? I needed to think about my approach.

The get-together was planned. Sue was about to head over for the evening, so that I could cook a meal and ease her into my concerns. She knew I had a dilemma, so there was some preparation for her mind. I didn't really want to give anyone else any trouble, but if this couldn't be shared, then I'd just crumble into loneliness! Sue arrived and we had a lengthy hug. She could sense I had ultimate issues of some sort. I didn't want to get into things straight away, so we shared some usual-life catch-up time while I prepared the food in the kitchen. We both shared a lovely wine. I needed relaxation between the two of us.

We eventually sat at the dinner table with a greatly prepared roast meal! I went to great lengths to ensure we could fill ourselves up for comfort.

Sue looked great. Her hair was long, curly and flowy, just as I always remembered it to be. Her skin was smooth and shiny, looking very healthy and well moisturised. I couldn't help notice her appearance, as I wondered how she would look *after* my strange confessions! She approached the subject with bravery, wanting to know what this meal was all about.

"So come on then Jen, give me the gen!" She took a large gulp of wine.

I knew we couldn't skim around the subject anymore, but I didn't want her to choke on her food!

"Well, I lost a nice chap I was dating."

"Ah, man trouble. I can handle that."

I cringed and worried about what she *could* handle!

"Well, there's a lot more to it, but I just can't keep this kind of thing to myself. It's so frightening."

Sue looked concerned, taking another heavy gulp of her wine and tucking into a load of mashed potato.

"Come on then. Let's talk through it."

I couldn't taste my food through fear of her expected reaction.

"Okay, well, you might want to avoid putting anything into your mouth right now."

"Ooh!" Sue was joking, "I'm sure whatever it is, we can get through this."

She used the word "we". I liked that.

"Well, you see, something weird happened to my arm, which left me with a strange ability. It's a very strange thing, so I want you to be prepared."

Sue frowned. Something nobody would expect anyone to say! She avoided putting any food into her mouth.

"You see, I don't know how exactly, but after a strange night of weird dreams, I woke up with a sore arm."

I could see that Sue was expecting something simple and ridiculous by her given expression.

"Well, spit it out before I spit my food out."

Sue was honest and waiting patiently. It was enough to make me feel confident that she was strong.

"I... have this strange ability to breathe through my arm when I'm under water. Like a fish!"

Sue looked as if she was going to roll about laughing, but let out a humorous tut.

"What?" She was leaning forward with interest.

"It's true! I had this weird dream that some doctor injected something into my arm, and then since that night my arm is able to open up slightly and behave just like a fish gill!"

Sue laughed harder than I've ever seen her laugh, occasionally wrapping her lips over the wine glass to gulp a few heavy mouthfuls.

"Well, I didn't cope with it well to start with, so I wouldn't expect you to believe it straight away."

Sue frowned now, realising I was serious.

"I guess that's a difficult one to share with a doctor!"

I wasn't sure if Sue was taking me seriously, or if she was analysing my mind.

"I believe what you're saying is very real to you. I just don't know what to say. It sounds very strange!"

"I don't want to be a test subject Sue, but I feel like in some ways I have already been one. I'm starting to wonder if I should fill my entire house with cameras. But then I think what's done is already done and that perhaps someone is observing me, like I'm in some kind of fish bowl!"

"Fish bowl? Ha-Ha!" Sue was certainly seeing the funny side, which I didn't mind at all. "So you think you might be part of some kind of experiment?"

"I wouldn't be surprised. I just don't know how to cope with the odd abilities. I've discovered two or three of them so far. One is the fish gill; the other is webbed feet and hands and unbelievable strength! I may even have greater hearing abilities."

I noticed Sue's face drop. She looked down at my hands and then up at my face.

"But your hands look perfectly fine."

This was the time I knew she may think I was losing my marbles.

"Sue, the abilities come when they are needed. At least that's how I'm seeing it. The gill pops up when I'm in water, and the feet and hand thing happens when I'm ... well... When I was sexually excited! This is when I was super strong too!"

I could see Sue's eyes thinking.

"So is this why you have the man trouble too? Did he see all of this? Is this why you are in some kind of danger? Will they take you in to experiment on you do you think?"

Now, I was the one getting a little worried for Sue, as I could tell she was taking me seriously, but worried about what might happen to me.

"No, no. I'm okay Sue. The chap I was seeing didn't witness anything unusual other than the fact I was a bit too strong for the average lady."

The table went quiet for a while. Sue was sinking into her glass more and was almost out of wine. I grabbed the bottle and poured more in for her. She didn't look comfortable now. Her humour had slipped away and her thoughts were elsewhere, perhaps planning her escape from the madness, or even the house. The silence lasted a few minutes and the drink flowed between us.

"I know this is a heck of a lot to digest. I'm living in a strange time right now." I wanted to break the silence.

Sue continued with the silence and kept her eyes down, mostly taking big gulps of her wine. By now, she would certainly need to stop here for the night, unless she was so desperate that a Taxi was in order.

"I just don't know Jen. I really don't know. Is this definitely real?"

"I'm sorry to say so. The only person I could turn to was you. I didn't want to bring any stress to you, but you're the only person. I can't tell my own mother. She wouldn't cope, but I wouldn't cope keeping it all to myself. I don't expect you to do anything except allow me to share my story so that I don't feel alone."

I could see her digesting the words.

"Ah, Jen, I'm so sorry you're part of something so really bloody weird. This isn't bloody normal."

I was starting to see the funny side of her chosen words.

"I want to show you what happens to my arm, as I know that water activates it, but I don't want to frighten you. It's just important for me to know that you're here for me in some shape or form. I know it's a lot of pressure."

I could tell Sue believed me enough without seeing *anything*.

"What are we going to do then Jen? Maybe you could be like Superman, use the abilities and have an alter-ego."

I could see a glimmer in Sue's eyes now. She was always good at seeking a good mind-set over every event.

"I guess I could." The thought made me chuckle. I would need to be a hero of the water life.

"Does it give you any pain though? You seem pretty calm considering this is the weirdest frigging thing I've ever heard!"

I smiled with her words.

"The arm throbs a bit when wanting to change structure."

Sue's expression changed again.

"Ah come on! This really can't be real! You're going to have to show me now."

"Shit. I don't know if you're ready. It made me faint when I first witnessed it properly!"

"I don't give a crap. Run a bath, or whatever you need to do. If you can take it, then I think I can."

I looked at our plates.

"Don't you want to finish eating first?"

"Do you think I feel like bloody eating now?"

At least she has always been the honest type of person.

Darn it, she is going to faint!

"Okay, well could you please have a bit more wine first? You're still too sober."

Sue gulped her wine down and finished it, lifting her glass up to request more. I complied with the pouring and sat uncomfortably, watching her force another load into her body.

"Okay, let's do this!" She sounded ready.

I was as nervous as hell thinking about how she might react.

The water poured into the bath and I felt my arm begin to throb as it did a few times before. Sue watched me cringing with the throbbing. I held my arm in the water, ready to witness the change again. I noticed Sue's eyes were slightly glazed over from the alcohol, which is what I wanted.

The vein that sits in the crease of my elbow grew larger and then began splitting the skin into two parts. I wondered how the vein coped with that for a moment! Why the vein, when that would surely burst with blood?

Either way, I could see the two parts forming, to shape into "flaps", leaving a large, open shape in the middle, where the motion gave the impression of breathing. The gap was just a deep, black hole in my arm! I was watching my arm so much, that I forgot to look up at Sue. She looked rather pale, but couldn't stop looking intensely. We were both quiet for this time.

I pulled my arm back out into the dry but didn't want to touch it with the towel. I don't know why. It just looked too gross to touch!

I couldn't believe Sue's words, but they helped!

"It looks like an alien fanny!"

I laughed slightly and noticed her shock was turning to laugher. She couldn't seem to stop laughing. It helped release the stress for both of us. The laugher grew between us and we walked wearily back into my dining area, where we just giggled and continued to drink. We were a complete wreck of alcohol and stress relief.

The next morning we must have looked like a couple of train wrecks. I felt as if I had been here before when I woke to find the two of us crashed on the sofa. I just hoped we didn't film anything this time! Imagine that!

Sue woke shortly after me, panicking about having *really* weird dreams. I needed to remind her that the "arm event" was *actually* real. She recalled everything slowly and then began to act really strangely. I couldn't blame her, as it wasn't an everyday occurrence.

"Ah shit. I've been here all night, got completely sloshed and I'm meant to be attending a meeting today. How the hell am I meant to concentrate?"

I didn't know what to say, but I tried something.

"Fancy a coffee?" I was making a fresh one for myself.

I could tell Sue wasn't in a very happy state, but thankfully she accepted the coffee offer.

We both sat, trying to recalibrate our brains and bodies.

"What can we do Jen? This isn't normal." She rubbed her forehead.

"You're telling me! I have to live with it." I didn't mean to sound competitive.

Sue thought for a moment.

"What if you don't have to live with it? Maybe there is some scientist you could see."

"I will not be made to be some kind of lab experiment."

"You said you *think* you are already being experimented on somehow, so maybe seeing someone will at least give you someone that could literally work *with* you on it."

Sue had an encouraging thought.

"How would I find such research scientists though?"

"I was thinking... I know someone, who knows someone who is actually a scientist. Maybe they could point us in the right direction."

I was starting to feel guilty about dragging Sue into this whole situation now. Her complexion was really bad this morning, drink or no drink.

She turned to face me head-on now with a softer expression.

"Jen, I think this is up to you entirely. It's not fair for me to tell you what you should do." Her eyes had more feeling in them now.

"Thanks Sue. I'm really sorry to involve you. Maybe that was wrong. Just I didn't know who else to turn to."

"Ah Jen, I am so glad you involved me. I would hate for you to go through this alone. I'm your friend. It's what we do."

I handed her a piping hot coffee. We sat comfortably together for a while in our own thoughts.

Sue was the first to move, placing her drink down in front of her. "Now, I'm going to have to get going. There's a lot for me to do today, so I've got to get myself together. I want you to call me every day, okay? I'll come and see you again when I have another couple of days free, just in case we need some drink!"

Sue smiled at the thought of getting drunk over further occurrences.

I nodded with guilt and we both moved to start getting ourselves ready for the day.

Sue looked relatively good once again after being in the bathroom for some time. I think *I* still looked the same!

We needed to say our goodbyes, as Sue usually had a heavy work schedule. She was normally much worse with over-working than I have *ever* been and that's really saying something.

I wasn't sure what to do with myself that day. I looked at my hands, trying to figure out what provokes the webbed behaviour. In my head, the thought of it was ridiculous.

My phone was going crazy with calls and texts. I noticed Jack hadn't sent anything, which didn't surprise me. I guess I needed to accept that we wouldn't see one another again.

Jason was sending encouraging messages to entice me to get in touch.
James at work admitted he missed me being there, as things were beginning to build up quite considerably.
I was going to ensure I took the full time however, as obviously I had some things to work out. I know I was undecided about work, but now I needed personal time more than ever!

Karen was asking if it was time for another girlie get-together, as they were all agreeing it was good for us all.
At least I knew I was loved and needed. That was my greatest gift during all of this.

I needed to do something to distract myself for now. Making a special lunch for myself seemed like a good idea. I seemed to be amazingly driven at this point, just by focussing on something. I pulled out a few vegetables and chopped them up really swiftly, throwing them into a pot. I guess it was turning into some kind of stew or soup! It was random.

I needed onion. The skin came off and I chopped it into the tiniest pieces – something I've never done before. I slipped at one point and caught my finger, but the knife bounced back up, not hurting me at all!

Was that my imagination? Did I want to risk doing that again to see?

Shit, I'll try that again gently. I pushed the knife down, but it didn't slice through any skin!

Uh, brave!

My finger seemed rubbery.

Naa!

I tried again and noticed the knife bounced up, off my skin.

Naaaaaa!

I have rubbery skin now?

I took a big risk and threw the knife into my finger. It bounced up and avoided any damage. I looked at the knife and checked it over. I cut through parts of the onion again and it was certainly working. It was certainly sharp!

I'm invincible! No way!

I placed the knife down and recalled a few words Sue had said. Perhaps the alter-ego is the way to go, but of what use is it in this world of technology? Maybe I could just have some fun with it… take some crazy risks. Having fun could go to the ultimate level! I was pleased with the way my mind was coping in such a joyful light now. All thanks to nearly chopping my finger off!

Now then, what can I do to use all of my strange abilities?

Speaking of which, I suddenly remembered that my hearing was better than Jack's. Perhaps I could test the enhanced hearing ability out.

I took a step outside my front door and listened in to anything I wouldn't normally be able to hear.

Zoning into Patrick's house, I could hear some low murmuring of a conversation. Honing in even more so, I could pinpoint exact words!

I then looked to the ground to hear the feet of insects, tip-tapering about! Gosh, I need to switch this ability off! It's too much to be dealing with constantly. How bloody useful though!

I went back into my home, forgetting about the soup or stew I was in the middle of making.

I wanted to test my strength out now though, putting all cooking aside. The garden was still looking at me with temptation to get it in a good condition.

Okay then!

I grabbed a couple of tools from my shed and began pruning some rose bushes back, followed by some other bushes. A stronger pair of cutters trimmed back some branches from a tree in the middle. Somehow I managed to jump up enough to reach some difficult-to-reach branches higher up.

I grabbed my lawnmower and trimmed the grass; the strimmer tidied up the edges for me. The job was done within a few minutes. It was quite a large garden, so perhaps doing things together in bulk got it together quickly.

I stood to admire the work.

Just as I was packing away, I felt eyes on me. Looking around I noticed Patrick looking through the window, noticing me noticing him! He gave me a thumbs-up as if to approve of the work. I know he was a keen gardener. Looking over at his garden, I could see that it was most likely, in fact, his pride and joy.

I sat on my little bench, which looks out over the garden, just contemplating and admiring my good work. It was difficult to see how the changes in my abilities would affect my life. I knew relationships would be out of the question, unless somebody could accept that I was bloody weird! Why would Jack or Jason want to be with someone who was some kind of Amphibian? I knew Jack was a goner for me, but hey, I did hurt the poor chap. No man wants his bits to be super painful!

Lots of thoughts went around my head. Some were amazingly useful thoughts, such as how I might be able to surf without ever worrying about drowning, or perhaps even being able to climb up the side of walls with my suction pads! It was strange to compare myself to someone like Spiderman, or some bizarre superhero! I wasn't sure what true use all of these gifts would bring however, they were the type of abilities you'd want to hide!

This holiday has been the strangest situation I have ever encountered in my life. I think it would be anyone else's nightmare situation! Poor Sue though; my worry for her increased. It wasn't something you could digest within an hour or two.

For a moment it seemed easier to hide away for the rest of my life, but then I snapped myself out of that idea before it set in! Life was to be lived! Perhaps this is the fun I was looking for! Perhaps this will enhance my life! I needed to play with this idea.
I thought on for quite a few hours, allowing time to slip by accidentally.

The evening came and I decided to drink yet another large glass of wine. I would need to stock up again on that soon! It wasn't normal for me to drink so much however. Control was needed. Just one more night! It's needed right now to settle my nerves.
I went to bed and fell asleep in a dash!

The next morning I woke with a revelation. I would document every event! I'm not sure why this would be a good idea, but it felt like the right thing to do.

Breakfast was a bit strange this morning because I really craved a load of eggs and fish! I would usually eat something relatively light first thing, to get things moving! Fish though?
I found some eggs in the fridge and cooked up an omelette of a strange combination, just to attempt to fulfil my cravings. It seemed to work. I was so hungry, but then I remembered my lack of food the day before. That soup or stew was never prepared!

On this morning I decided to head over to the beach for a second attempt at the surfing! The only thing was that I needed to buy another surf board.

I collected myself and my belongings; checked my phone and emails and then jumped into the car. It was early in the morning, so many were still fast asleep.

I escaped most of the traffic on the way down. I was hoping most people would be working on this day anyway.
On the way down, I decided to stop off at a shop to gather some flowers and chocolates. I needed to visit the fuel station that helped me in the neediest of times.

I arrived at the fuel station and offered my gifts, thanking the lady profusely for her previous rescue! At first she didn't recognise me, which was a compliment in itself. I certainly wasn't in the same messy pickle during our first interaction. When she *did* recognise me, she was just extremely happy to see me looking so well! She had a few moments to ask about my car situation, which I could only report as being the same, with insurers still on the case.
I passed on my appreciation to her colleague, Andy too.
They both had too many customers at one point, which was my cue to leave. I decided to leave my business card with them should *they* ever need anything *I* could help with.

I left, feeling content with my behaviours of gratitude and picked up the rest of my journey to the beach.

I soon parked up in my usual car park and pulled everything out that I needed, with excitement.

The same surf shop was already open, with people outside, waxing their boards down and chatting about their exciting plans. It was a little bit intimidating for a starter and someone who was doing it alone. I knew a beginner taking dangerous risks wasn't the best thing! Yet here I was, talking to the same sales man about having my car and surf board stolen. He looked at me with doubt, as if I was making up some elaborate excuse for losing the board, perhaps in the sea. The more I tried to tell him that it was a true situation, the more I felt he was nodding in a "yeah-yeah" kind of way!

I decided not to care and to ask for the same type of board, since it did slide into my car and it was good for beginners to use, apparently!

He complied with a grin of continual disbelief, asking me if I needed a new tub of board wax. I reminded him that *everything* went with the stolen car.

If I was going to surf around these parts frequently, then I didn't really want the locals to think I was some kind of elaborate story teller! Imagine their thoughts on the Amphibian circumstances! I'd certainly be an outcast!

I decided to take my new gift to the edge of the sand, so that I could find a decent space and place of privacy to prepare this new board. Surfing was something I really wanted to practice and excel in. It was always something that intrigued me. I could quite happily watch the men in their wetsuits riding the waves for hours too! But it wasn't about the gender, it was admiring the skill. I rarely saw the ladies out there, but perhaps I could find a surfer buddy in good time.

I felt good, getting myself and the board prepared, walking onto the sand now, setting up camp with my towel and small bag. I stripped down to my bikini, enjoying the sun kissing my skin already. It was another beautiful day.

At first I was nervous about my arm showing up with the weird gill thing. It started to throb as I grew nearer the water. I begged my body not to change, as there were too many people around. I couldn't disguise it as anything else. Perhaps I should have purchased the wetsuit!
As I stepped into the shallow parts, the gill started to open up.
No!
Okay, I guess I need to buy a darn wetsuit.

I headed back to the same surf shop and requested some assistance with the correct fit and type. The gentleman looked a little less judgemental this time and complied with a smile on his face.
This was even more exciting though! My own wetsuit! Another bonus would be keeping my boobs hidden!

I was in the water with many other swimmers and surf or body boarders. It felt great to be part of the fun and excitement of the good weather.

After hundreds of attempts of jumping up onto the board and trying to ride the smaller waves, I was starting to get the knack again. My legs were aching again, but I still felt strong. Others were doing extremely well and I noticed kids body-boarding with many chuckles along the way.

I was going for it at one stage and got a little bit too cocky. A big brute of a man came crashing along on his surfboard, but I was getting into his space accidentally, obviously with my lack of experience. He hit my board hard, knocking me off, causing me to land hard on the water awkwardly. At first, I didn't even have time to realise what had happened. Suddenly I was under water, trying to figure out *where* I was in the water. At first I thought I was upside down. It was confusing trying to figure it out with waves lapping over me!

I felt the gill on my arm trying to flap about under the tight wetsuit.

The strap keeping my ankle attached to the surfboard came to mind, so I pulled at it to see where the board was. I looked at the way the attachment was moving, to figure out which direction was up. Why did I have to get knocked over in the deep parts? I was certainly getting way too ahead of myself.

I felt as if I was spinning around and around, trying to gain some control. Just as I thought I was starting to figure it out, I banged my head on something above, something really big and hard. It knocked me for six. In fact, I know my mind went blank for a moment and that I must have drifted further away. Strangely, I wasn't panicking now. Everything felt calm and tranquil. This calm was needed to get me thinking straight. I felt a hard and sharp pull on my ankle. My leg was now being dragged through the water. An arm tucked under my body and allowed my head to filter up to the surface. A face looked down at me with much concern. I realised I was being carried by some amazing action man onto land. He placed me down and felt the side of my neck. "I'm okay!" I mustered.

The man frowned and appeared put-out for being stopped in his tracks.

"But you must've been under for at least five minutes!"

He had some kind of Australian accent. It was very appealing. His words struck me and I wondered how long I was actually under the water for! Perhaps he *was* right! The strange fish-gill must have saved my oxygen levels.

I came to my current view and noticed the many water droplets sitting on top of a finely crafted set of pectorals. This man's chest was wonderfully sexy! Trying not to make it obvious that I was staring, I noticed his abs were also very nice and chiselled!

Ooh what a dream.

I slowly crouched to climb up onto my feet. The man held his hands outright, attempting to capture any stumble I may have.

"Honestly, I am truly okay."

I suddenly realised my lack of gratitude.

"Oh my goodness, how rude of me; I must be a bit dazed, as I haven't told you how grateful I am! Thank you so much for saving me!"

Uncharacteristically, I hugged him intensely with the words.

He was so firm that it was like hugging a tree! He didn't respond physically, but was hinting verbally that it was okay to let go.

"Okay, okay. It's all okay. You're okay, which is the main thing."

I released him from my arm chains and stepped back with slight embarrassment.

"Sorry. I just wanted to naturally express my gratitude."

He lifted a hand as if to say "stop".

"Yeah, it's totally fine. I just saw you go down and then a careless person go over your area with some cheap, wooden boat. I wasn't sure if it hit you or not."

That made sense! A boat... A silly boat!

I felt my head and it felt a little bit tender, but not too bad.

"*Did* he hit your head then?"

I gave a thin grin with the realisation that a boat *did* hit me.

"It did!"

"Ah, then maybe we should get you to a lifeguard who can get you checked over."

"No, no... I remember the bump, but it's fine. I can tell it was more of a graze. I won't waste anyone's time knowing I'm actually okay."

"Well just be careful and watch out for any signs or symptoms that aren't quite right."

What does *he* know about signs or symptoms that aren't quite right?! I can't tell him of *my* unusual ones!

I looked at his eyes. Wow! He had piercing eyes! What a perfect man.

"Well, I will leave you in peace, but if you get back in the surf, please be careful of arrogant men who think their surf path is theirs. Or perhaps just keep away from other surfers while you're learning. There's plenty of space in the sea for you to have a nice patch to practise."

Ooh, his accent was just to die for.

"Well, thank you for the advice. I guess you can tell I'm a beginner then."

He started to walk off, moving his bum so perfectly back towards the sea.

"Just be careful!" were his final offering of words in my direction.

He was right.

I felt quite a wally.

Perhaps the gill thing was created for me somehow to prepare for my careless fun days!

I sat for a while, attempting to unzip the wetsuit to gain some sunbathing time. A lady in another wetsuit came along, offering some help to get the zip down. It was awkward if you had slightly tight shoulders. I accepted willingly, since I was now in some kind of lethargic mood.

I didn't expect the lady to speak, but she did!

"I noticed your efforts out there. You don't give up. That's what it's all about. You'll never master a skill if you don't keep at it. Practice, practice, practice... Don't let setbacks stop you. I fell off a million times and hurt myself multiple times. It's such an addiction though once you get better at it."

I appreciated her kindness whilst unzipping me!

"Thank you very much! That's good to know."

"Just one thing – when you do fall into the deep parts, cover your head like this, just in case the board is just above you. I learnt that after a few times of bumping my head."

She demonstrated her hands to sit on top of her head.

"That's good advice, thank you!"

It was so nice to know that people were so kind and helpful.

"I want to thank that chap so much. He would probably think I'm obsessive if I want to keep thanking him though!"

The lady laughed. I looked at her to notice she was around my age. That brought much comfort.

"I would let the chap go. Men come and go all of the time in this place."

"Do you live locally?" I couldn't help but wonder.

"I do. I love it here in the summers."

"Wow, my ultimate dream has always been to live by the coast."

"Well, what's stopping you?"

I thought for a moment.

"I think I let work conquer me completely. This is a little holiday for me. I rarely take holidays!"

"Oh girl, life is way too short to live around work."

I heard it many times, even in my own head over the years.

"Yeah I know. It's just amazing where the time goes before you *actually* realise these things."

"Well you must have your head screwed on to know what you're doing wrong and try to fix it at least."

This lady seemed wise. She did look a little bit too cool to be helping a random lady pull a zip down though. Her hair was long and wavy with perfect blonde shapes. The kind I would expect to be with the man who had just rescued me!

I know it shouldn't be about looks, but they are the type that would fit well together.

The lady could see I was with my thoughts, so said her goodbyes and walked back to her towel on the sand.

I started to fully remove the wetsuit, checking my arm carefully before exposing it. It was almost as if it was a life on its own on my body. At least that was how I was treating it, like an alien on my arm!

I managed to pull the wetsuit off all together without pulling any part of my bikini off. Successful first attempt in pubic! It was hard enough putting it on.

I sunbathed as planned, recalling the great surfing attempts despite the accident. It was worth it, even if it was only getting to see the amazing-looking surfers. It was noticeable that many of the young men had longer hair and that the ladies didn't seem to care about breaking their nails. I liked the perception of freedom that they gave. It was something I wanted for myself. Perhaps that was the kind of lifestyle I was seeking with all of this craving for fun.

I sunbathed for a while without much care, leaving the accident shock behind. After rolling around, turning regularly to get cooked on all sides, I noticed the heroic man walk up to me. I felt all funny, with butterflies inside.

"Hey, are you still feeling good?"

I still couldn't get past his amazing accent, let alone the perfectly shaped body.

The sun was almost shining through one of his shoulders, making him look as if he was glowing.

"I'm feeling great thanks! I'm still very grateful for your help. Have you done this kind of thing before?"

"What, saving people from drowning in the sea?"

"I guess that's what I'm asking."

I felt myself blush, hoping it may be camouflaged by some sun bathing colour!

This guy had enough courtesy to check on me. How amazing!

"Well, it's happened a couple of times when the shore has been a bit cluttered with various abilities."

"So I'm not the only plonker?"

He actually grinned and showed a softer side, dismissing the insult to myself.

"Hey, we're having a barbeque on the beach, just up there by that shed if you want to join us later," he pointed, "it's just a few surfers who like to get together and have some food, drink and a chat. I just thought you might fancy a bit of company if you're stopping long enough."

I couldn't believe what I was hearing!

"Oh, well, I guess I could. I was going to head back home, but how could I resist such an offer?"

"Great!" He grinned even broader!

Was this a date? Or was he just being kind?

I didn't want to ask just in case it messed up my confidence.

Sure enough, I noticed a little later on that people were starting to gather by the so-called shed. Some were already holding drinks and nattering away.

Oh, I really don't know if I could just walk up to a crowd and say "hello! I'm just joining you to eat your food and drink your drink!"
I thought I would wait for the familiar Australian figure to head up into the small crowd, so that I could at least have an introduction to people.

The sun started to get that nice evening feel to it, so I decided to place my clothes on over the bikini and place the chunky items back in the car. I couldn't quite hide the surfboard in the car however, risking another tempted thief.
Argh!

It was likely that I was going to join the crowd for some social interaction.
Jeepers, I really was going for it with the fun levels! I became very self-aware, looking at myself in the rear view mirror of the car to check my appearance over. I thought I looked pretty good considering the day in the sun and the sea water in my hair.
My hair was wavy and defined with the slight crust of salt. It looked sexy tilted more to one side of my head and going over the shoulder. I had waterproof make-up on, which really did enhance my eyes just right!
My guts were telling me not to do this however. I couldn't decipher between my nerves or my instincts. Reading books on

facing fears were popping into my head. If I face my fears with this, I could potentially have surfer friends!

So, this was my mind set. It was decided.

My legs felt wobbly, as I walked back from the car to the shed area near the beach. I couldn't yet see the familiar figure of a man that I should have asked the name of!

We certainly didn't think that part through! As I grew close to the small crowd, I had a plan to walk casually past, whilst looking out for the familiar figure. If he wasn't there, then I'd keep going until I found a place to buy a drink! That would be a useful idea anyway, to have a drink in my hand! I know it brings comfort to hold something between people.

I felt a tug on the crease in my right elbow as I tried to creep through casually.

"Hey, you made it! I was looking out for you."

Instant calm hit me, recognising his comforting accent.

"Ah, hello, I was just going to get a drink and head back."

He reached into a large iced bucket, pulling out a small bottle for me.

"No need. I invited you, so here you go."

"Thank you so much!"

This man seemed very kind. I still felt a little bit nervous however.

Be sociable, be sociable! I am confident. I truly am! I am adaptable to all new situations!

Mind talk...

It truly helps!

I tried to keep my voice stable, without wobbles. This group wasn't very large, perhaps about seven people, but they were all very cool. I know I can give off a perception of being cool, but I'm not sure that it's my true nature.

I observed the scene to see how things were pulled together for this gathering. I was stood close to a small, wooden, circular table that looked extremely well used.

Only a couple of steps away, some relaxed-looking men were standing over a homemade barbeque, turning the food over every now and then. Thankfully the smoke was blowing in the right direction, so I didn't have to worry about fighting through discomfort. Everyone seemed friendly and relaxed as a general rule. I was the one who needed to lighten up from all of my fussy thoughts.

"So where are you from?" I guess the nice Australian asked the obvious question.

"Oh, a couple of hours from here, a little place called Bray. Have you heard of it?"

"Nope, but a couple of hours seems far? So I guess this was meant to be a day trip?"

I sensed disappointment in his voice.

"Well, I don't have anything to rush back to, so I guess I'll just be going home for the bed when it's time."

"Ah, well make the most of the grub then. They're cooking plenty today. We have excess to use up tonight."

He pointed with his bottle, his accent sounding very strong.

Others standing around were looking comfortable in conversation.

"So, I don't know if I told you, I'm Jenny."

He reached his hand out very officially, which I complied with, to feel a very gentle handshake.

"Josh."

It felt like a brief introduction.

"So where do *you* live? I take it you're very local."

"Oh I'm just a ten minute drive up the road. A few of us have vans or campervans just in case we overdo things."

I instantly got the idea and grinned. He quickly continued, trying to keep a nice conversation between us.

"You should do the same ya know? Get a van or something so you can stop over if needed. It's great to hang around by the sea... See the sun go down and rise."

I thought about it for a moment.

"Well, I'm not being sexist towards myself or anyone else, but I don't think I'd feel too safe being a lady on my own, in a van. For me, I'd prefer a bed and breakfast place maybe."

I felt I was sounding a bit boring.

"Ah, you like ya comforts too?"

I cringed at his analysing.

"Oh no, I'm all up for the simple things. I guess I would just be a bit nervous being a single girl and all that."

I noticed a smile on his face.

"Well, we all park in the same crafty spot, away from any trouble. You just need to hang around with the right crowd."

"I guess you're right. I love the beach so much, but I didn't think about this kind of thing."

"So, you're new to surfing and stuff?"

"I am really. I love water, but it's usually limited to a good swim in a local pool. I fancied something different for a while. I fancy more fun in life. Summer's the best time to get out and do these things."

"Cool, well, we hang out here normally one evening a week to catch up, sometimes more. You can come and join us anytime."

I liked the open invite.

"Thanks."

We spoke for quite some time about the beach lifestyle and the freedom of their lives. He told me about some of his friends that were with us. Some of them had regular jobs and others made excuses not to work. I got to talk to a few of the people there and noticed the lady that I spoke to earlier was stood in the distance with the same group. She eventually came over for a chat, predictively mentioning our initial introduction. A proper introduction allowed a name exchange. I discovered her name was Annie. She didn't look like an Annie however. She asked me a lot of questions about what I did for a living and what kind of lifestyle I had. The financial work seemed to raise an eyebrow, as did my mention of the type of cars I drove. I wasn't trying to show off at all. In fact, I felt I was giving away how boring my life was compared to the crowd I was with. Despite that, Annie didn't seem to give a judging eye and I felt quite comfortable chatting with her.

I wasn't sure if I was being naïve or not, but I was beginning to fit in with the group with less effort after a couple of hours.
I'm not sure if they were trying really hard, or if I was just finding myself relax with them more.

There was a change in action within the group when it grew quite dark. Secret conversations appeared to move around them. I was considering my exit plan with a simple excuse at this point, but Annie began to explain their talks.

"You see that posh boat out there in the distance?"
"Yes."
"Well, they treat us pretty badly, like we're the scum of the Earth."
"Why would they do that? Do you go out *that* far?" It looked miles away.
Annie shrugged her shoulders and began telling me about an event.
"One day, a lot of us were surfing together and switched to hand paddling on our fronts when we got further out. I don't think they liked us low-life lot getting too close to the boat."
"Well, that's their problem."
"Well you'd think so, but someone on the boat decided to do some Scuba Diving and thought he owned the entire area. He came across one of our friends who apparently got in the way and just decided to push them off their board and cut his urethane cord with some huge hunting knife."
"Urethane cord?"
Annie noticed my confusion.

"You know… the cord that attaches from the board to the ankle?"

"Oh! Sorry. So what happened to your friend?"

"Well, they pushed him about, causing him to go deeper into the water. They didn't even have a motive, just pure aggression, unless their motive is to keep people away from their precious boat."

I was surprised to hear such a shocking thing.

Annie looked a bit sheepish though, strangely.

"We keep thinking about getting some form of revenge every time we see the boat."

I remembered my first impression of Annie was that she was wise and kind. Perhaps she didn't think the same way as I did about not fighting fire-with-fire.

"Did you not report them to the police?"

"We considered it, but thought they probably wouldn't do very much, if anything at all."

I wanted to give advice, but not to sound all prudish, so instead probed with a question that was out of character for me.

"So what kind of revenge has been going around your head?"

"Well, not just me, but a few of us, have thought about creeping onto their boat when they have their moonlight parties or snoozes."

"What would you do when you've gotten on the boat though?"

I worried about what kind of people I was now mixing with. They seemed nice, perhaps extremely loyal to one another. Thankfully I could ask these questions without any involvement, hopefully to gain some trust.

"Well, we would probably steal something reasonable. Not for the money, just for revenge."

"On surfboards? Isn't that tricky?"

"We're super experienced on our boards Jen. We don't know what kind of things they have on board, but it would be worth a little snatching revenge."

Annie was smiling now, with a little bit of hatred in her eyes. At least that was how her expression seemed.

There seemed to be a lot of scuffling and discussion going on within the group, with them talking slightly angrily and looking up at the boat.

I felt it was certainly a time for me to get going. This was a piece of revenge I couldn't be involved with.

I noticed the group looked as if they were getting geared up to go into the sea.

"Are they going for *this* revenge now?" I felt naïve with the question.

Annie looked guilty.

"You could come with us if you wish. They just want to take a closer look."

I definitely didn't want to get involved. I also didn't want to head back into the cold evening waters, when I'd been comfortably wearing my clothes!

"Ah, I'm thinking I should head back home. It's getting late and I have a two hour journey yet."

Annie looked down at my held bottle. I knew what she was thinking.

"Ah, I've only had this one. I know I'm legal to drive."

She turned one edge of her lip up.

"You can stay in my spare tent near my van tonight if you prefer to stay for a bit more fun."

I knew this would be going too far. The party was something different, but a novice surfer going into the sea in the dark was pushing it, let alone being involved in some crime!

"Oh come on Jenny! If you fancy a little surf with us, then head home afterwards if you prefer, then at least you can say you've even surfed in the night! I could stick near you if you need some support."

She was a pushy pair of britches, although her tone of words was quite encouraging. She was twisting my arm and I pouted with consideration. The pain was heading back for my board however.

"What about swimming after eating?"

My worries were becoming obvious.

Annie just gave a cool, calm smile and handed a supposed free surfboard into my hands. It was leaning comfortably on top of other surf boards, against a large pole.

"Who does that belong to?"

"It doesn't matter Jen. You've got to learn to chill out a little more. We have a big selection that gets chained up here. We sell these ones second hand."

"You sell second hand surfboards?"

"Why the heck not? It gets us some extra cash."

I wasn't sure if this lady was for real. My expression must have said it all.

"Look Jen, we rent the shed and sell stuff. We also sell surfboards that are chained up here. That's how we can have our little drinks here whenever we fancy."

It made sense. I could see Annie was detecting my judgement, but it didn't faze her. She seemed happy to give me full explanations. With her assumed honesty, it helped me to relax a bit.

"Oh, well now I understand what you guys do."

"Well, not all of us. It's only a small handful of us who take care of this little business. The chap who saved you is a really well paid guy doing some kind of software work. As you can see, it doesn't matter what we do, as we get on great and tend to stick together."

Her words made me feel like a bit of an outsider, but it was nice to hear more detail.

She grabbed her own surfboard and threw me a random wetsuit.

"I can help you with the zip if you like?"

I laughed with slight embarrassment.

"I guess I've got to figure this stuff out eventually."

I decided to join in on the preparation, trying to keep up with their experienced speed!

It seemed the fun thing to do after all; to have a bit of daring time with people who appeared to be loyal and friendly.

"Yes! You're in!" Annie seemed very excited about my decision.

Before I knew it, I was having a bit of a panic, wading through the sea in the pitch black. I felt my arm pulsate hard, with the knowledge that it was transforming in the water again!

It was so dark, and the only thing with light was the boat in the deeper part of the sea. Annie kept using her voice for me to follow her. I kept my fear to myself, since I wasn't close enough to have my breathing noises heard!

What the hell was I getting myself into now? So far, the crazy fun was finding me!

Everyone appeared to congregate in a large circle with their boards and I did my best to hold my board as controlled as possible. Annie was occasionally able to reach out to tug me closer. I probably looked like a needy idiot compared to these skilled surfers. There seemed to be some kind of sign language going on from one of the bigger members. I noticed him earlier in the evening, as his arms were pretty big. His hair cut was almost completely shaven on the sides, but almost Mohican on top, just a little wider. It was quite a smart style really! Very sharp!

He gave some hand signals that I didn't understand, but everyone else seemed to grasp immediately.

They all went off paddling with their arms on their surfboards, deeper into the sea.

Annie looked at me and encouraged me to follow.

I didn't feel comfortable and looked back with temptation to scramble to the shore.

"It's okay Jen, we're just heading deeper. I'll keep a good eye on you if you just keep close."

She was instinctive, so I gave a little trust.

The water felt lovely in fact and the board seemed to float so peacefully over the top. There were very flat waves, almost flat enough to skim over the top of. We were all lying on our boards anyway, just paddling with our arms, so it wasn't like trying to ride the waves on our feet.

As I looked only a short distance ahead of me, I didn't notice how close that boat was getting to us!

"Shit!" I realised they were *definitely* tempted to do something in revenge!

"Annie! No! I'm not going to be part of any revenge crime!"

"Shush," she said without further explanation.

I turned to head back, but she shouted back at me in a loud whisper.

"Jenny, we're just having a look, that's all. It's just a sneaky adventure, okay? Have some fun!"

She didn't know the half of it! Here I was, my arm pulsating and trying to breathe through the wet suit and Annie was advising me to have some fun!

We grew so close to the boat that I knew we were taking a major risk. It was strangely insightful however to see how boats *did* look when in the water, so close to them!

It was so dark, but I could make out the shape and power of this boat. It appeared to be so shiny and smooth that I wanted to touch it! Annie told me to get closer, but it made me feel nervous.

"What if they get the boat moving?" I whispered.

"Don't worry they always seem to anchor here for hours over night for a few nights at a time. I think they have water holidays or something."

I paid attention to the lovely flapping water noises, while we gently floated around the area of the boat. The people on the boat must have been really relaxing, or asleep, as there didn't appear to be any noises coming from it at all.

My arm "gill" was trying to do things underneath my wetsuit, but I did my best to ignore it and carry on.

What was I doing?

Despite my concerns about this event I decided to take part in, it was quite exciting and tranquil, coming out to surf in the dark, with much calmer waves. We were in quite a deep part of the sea for the boat to be gently rocking now. I was impressed with my bravery.

Annie seemed to care about me, like a new child at school. I suppose it is very similar!

Despite the darkness, the side of the boat seemed to shimmer with a nice silver colour, which made me notice the dark figure of one of the surfers attempting to climb a side ladder onto the boat!

"Annie, no, this isn't what I came out to do! I should have known! What are you planning to do?" I was shouting in a low pitch, to attempt to keep the noise down.

"Shush, it's okay, he's just going to have a look. We said we would see what kind of things they get up to. We can't understand why the scuba diver wanted to frighten us away. They must be up to something."

I couldn't believe it.

"Even so, you aren't the police... and this is a crime!"

"Jen, just chill the hell out. *You're* only out here for the surf. *We* won't take part in the little bit of spying."

"I'm heading back!" I turned to paddle away with my little hands.

"Jenny!" She tried to whisper loudly without anyone hearing.

I didn't care. It wasn't my drama and I didn't want my fun to be about going to prison! I seemed to be able to paddle fast all of a sudden, so paid attention to my hands, to notice the webbed fingers had returned! I also felt immensely strong again!

Woohoo! This was now becoming useful!

With my distraction however, I didn't notice one of the male surfers sat on his board observing from further out. He moved in front of my direction and grabbed the front of my board, causing both of us to have extreme wobbles. He fell in, making me worry about him. I shouldn't have worried however as this wasn't something I chose to be involved in.

I felt a strong hand tilt my board over, causing me to slip sideways into the water!

The surfer attempted to pull me down into the water with him. He then pushed me deep into the water and rescued himself with a swift float back to the surface.

I somehow noticed from deep down, that he was grabbing my surfboard and attempting to take both of the boards for some reason! I then heard him speak to himself.

"Shouldn't have involved the silly cow!"

His voice sounded really hard and nasty.

I was beginning to resurface, when I heard Annie's voice shouting from a distance.

"Chris, what the hell are you doing?"

"Taking our board back! What use is she to us? She's just a novice surfer who's going to drag us down."

I lowered myself beneath the surface of the water, somehow able to breathe and hear everything. My hearing and eyesight was particularly strong. I couldn't understand it. The water was salty, with being the sea, so it should hurt my eyes! At the time, my adrenaline was pumping hard, but I wanted to hold tight and observe for a moment.

"She's useful to us Chris, you idiot! Where is she?"

"*How* is she useful to us? She can't surf for shit!"

"It's an extra pair of hands, with a bit of intellect."

"A bit of intellect isn't what we need right now."

"Of course it is! People like you make stupid mistakes like this! Now where the hell is she? Help me find her!"

Annie sounded upset. I sensed her placing herself in the water, trying to search for me. I looked up and could see her perfectly well through the surface water. She really did want me to be part of this team, but I needed to know their true actions.

For some reason I took it upon myself to swim swiftly back to the boat area. I wanted to observe their actions. With my ability to see and hear well, whilst I could swim with great power, I thought it would be the best opportunity to spy on them!

I was amazed at my speed and stealth. It wasn't explainable, but I didn't care at the time. I wanted answers to their behaviours. If this whole thing was a darned unusual dream, then it was certainly the most adventurous thing anyone could ever dream of.

The surfers were scattered around, keeping a good eye in extreme quiet. I felt like some kind of Ninja, creeping around, hoping not to be seen. Poor Annie was back in the ocean somewhere, trying to find me. I'll see how this pans out first, to see what kind of people they *truly* are.

I managed to get back to the boat in no time at all. I crept to the opposite side of the boat, away from all of the surfer's views.
There was a ladder on this side too.
I managed to get to this ladder but wondered how webbed feet were supposed to grip around each step! Awkward!
I touched the side of the boat for a split second, just to notice that my hand had suctioned itself in place!
Oh yes! I have some kind of sticky suction bloody Spiderman thing!
This was going to be a useful tool.
I found myself climbing up the side of the boat like some kind of giant lizard! As I reached the edge of the top, I had a sneak peak of the layout. It seemed much bigger than it was from the outside.
I found myself crawling into the boat and on the ground – again, like some bloody giant lizard!
This was too weird!
I crept around, noticing two people lying out on sun beds at the far end of the boat, looking as if they were star gazing. That was good. I just hoped that my lizard-like movements were quiet enough to snoop around.

What I would personally describe as a cabin, was like a small house that just slotted nicely into a boat shape! It seemed very posh and well kept. There were small blue spotlights, highlighting the walking areas and some less scattered lights above, on wood effect ceilings. I wanted a boat like this!

The first open-planned area had an amazing sofa, with matching chairs in a sparse area. This was quite good fun, taking a look around someone's posh boat! I did wonder where the naughty surfer had gone however. Wherever he was, he was doing a good Ninja job! I definitely witnessed him climbing on board.

As I crept about, I felt a little less comfortable about it. I was suddenly grovelling on my knees and slapping my hands on the floor. I looked down to notice my hands had returned to normal. The unusual strength still felt as if it was active however! It was perhaps a good idea for me to get up on my feet now, which was much more comfortable at this point!

I looked back to note the two people remaining on their sun loungers.

What a life!

There was an option of things now. I could see that there was a small staircase at the end of this section that sat perfectly central, leading upwards. There were doors either side of this staircase. I decided to feel one of the door handles to see where this directed me. Thankfully the door opened quietly, leading to a huge control system. It looked a little bit like a space ship's control centre. I realised both of the doors came into this space. I looked out of the windows that sat directly ahead and noticed that this must have been the front part of the boat. I knew nothing about boats! This meant I needed to attempt the staircase, since I discovered the main areas of the boat. I remembered the words of Annie. She mentioned my intelligence. Perhaps my current actions weren't so intelligent. Perhaps I didn't do anything intelligent since taking this holiday! I was certainly doing some very silly and risky things! As I found the staircase, I carefully placed one foot on the bottom step, praying they weren't creaky at all!

Thankfully, the first step felt very solid.

I managed to get to the top of these steps, to find the most amazing bedroom layout. The only question on my mind at this point now however, was the whereabouts of the surfer that climbed up onto the boat! I had covered all bases... I was certain of it!

I looked out of the windows to see if I could see any movement from another outlook. Everything seemed still and calm. Even the surfers were camouflaged in the dark waters. It took me a few seconds to notice a slight glimmer of one of the boards. At least I knew they were still out there waiting for something.

This was odd. I needed to see what this was all about.

I carefully took myself down the staircase again, looking outward from the sheltered rooms, right out to the open deck. Nothing had changed.

From walking out of the sheltered areas, I looked around the edge of the walls, to notice a small walkway around the circumference of the boat. If the surfer was still on the boat, then this was the last walking space that he could possibly be hanging around in, unless there was another layer to this gorgeous thing!

I walked cautiously around each turning point, but no-one was to be seen.

It wasn't until I started making my way back to find the little ladder that I caught sight of a head slipping down the opposite ladder!

I tried to increase my pace without making a noise. This opposite ladder was close now, so I peered over the edge to catch sight of the surfer holding onto some shiny items, trying to tuck them into a little black bag of some sort with one hand. He was hovering on the ladder at only a few steps down, enough to have his head tucked out of sight.

Was he stealing jewellery? That's what it certainly looked like. Annie mentioned revenge in theft. Was it revenge at all, or was it just knowing that there was something valuable on this boat? Why was I being encouraged to join in with this crime? They have enough big boys in the team to do it well together. Annie mentioned intelligence being needed, but there was the nice looking man who had a great job in software! He's intelligent! This didn't make sense!

I decided to watch the team of surfers as much as I could from my view over the edge of the boat. The "thieving" surfer gave a big "thumbs up" and was able to regroup, after someone returned his surfboard to his hands. The big man with the sharp hairstyle actioned everyone to head back to the shore swiftly. That part was obvious, as they all paddled hard with their hands in that direction. I looked back at the couple, still lying on their sun loungers. Their heads would occasionally turn to face one another very casually.

It was obvious that they were people with an abundance of money. One of their hands dangled over the edge of the bed, allowing me to catch detail of some expensive jewellery. There were a few golden bangles and rings just on that one arm! I had the impression of an older couple, with their shapes and hair colours from the view I had.   It was difficult to envision either one of them scuba diving, let alone committing any form of violence. Either someone else must be part of their team, or their appearance isn't as it seems.

Look at me, trying to play the detective!

I needed to leave the boat before I was spotted! The surfers were well on their way back to shore now. I'd need to swim back, hoping the amazing webbed feet and hands would activate! My arm felt normal at this particular time, but I assumed that it was because I needed to be in water for it to function again.

I actually loved these strange features about me now and wondered why I hadn't gone into a complete melt down about it. The whole thing was really bizarre, but amazing at the same time. I was some kind of monster, but in a useful way!

I crept down the ladder of the boat, re-entering the freezing cold water! It seemed to have grown extremely cold really fast. My arm pumped with the "mutation!"

At first I panicked in the vast sea, feeling very vulnerable, but as soon as I began to attempt my swim, I felt my hands and feet convert to their strange webbing! The strength appeared too, and I was able to move swiftly just under the surface of the water. I didn't seem to need to breathe through my mouth and nose, strangely.

I paddled with all fours like some crazy machine, rushing through as speedily as a speed boat! No surfers were about. I think I gave them plenty of return-time. I certainly didn't want to bump into them looking how I imagined I looked!

My hands grinded through some sand, making me realise I had already reached the shore. I lifted my head, seeing the vast beach and the surfers walking casually back up to the shed to congregate again.

This was now a time of decision. I remained on all fours, just allowing the shallow wave to lap over my legs and arms, giving me time to think.

The issue I had was Annie's peace of mind, to see that I was alive and well, but I didn't want to come across the man who pulled me into the water! Somehow I needed Annie alone for one moment of time. My alternative thinking was to just leave the entire situation, leaving them to worry about their consequences. My mind was divided and I struggled to make the decision.

I started to crawl on all fours on the sand and noticed that I could move equally fast on land! Maybe I was some kind of mixed Amphibian creature. I needed some answers on that, but I suppose the experiences would hopefully give me more knowledge.

It felt odd however, crawling fast on all fours, feeling a bit like some kind of strange idiot!

As I moved up slightly closer, it was dark enough not to be seen in the black wetsuit. I couldn't handle the thought of mingling with the crowd again. This was obviously my instinctive decision at this point.

I began to feel normal again in my body. My hands and feet had returned to their normal state and my arm felt comfortable. Disappointingly, I noticed my eyesight returning to normal vision. This shouldn't bring disappointment, but my normal eyesight wasn't as advanced as the "mutated" version! I felt disadvantaged now! Perhaps I was warming to my new features more and more!

I crept away, now in a safe place enough to stand up and run back up towards my car. Just as I approached, I noticed someone leaning against it!

Ah no! Now what?

I instantly stopped and crouched down to view the figure, hoping that they would move along. The figure was clearly Annie!

Ah man! How did she know it was my car?

Then I realised that I did explain the car type I was currently driving. There was also the possibility that she noticed me walking to and from that car park area. I also realised that their local knowledge was strong, so it shouldn't be surprising to me. I wondered how long she was going to wait there. If she was this observant generally, then she may have even spotted me already.

Argh! I just need to go and face the music.

I decided to stand in a really conspicuous way and start walking up to the direction of my car. At least she was alone, which was what I kind of wished for initially. I worried about how she may react to me approaching my car instead of returning to the group. Heck, it was my decision anyway!

There was no need to worry at all though, as she ran over to give me the biggest, loving hug!

Hey?

"I truly thought you were gone!" were her first words.

She pushed back to inspect my face.

"I'm fine. I just swam back to shore."

She looked remorseful.

"I am so sorry about that twit who hurt you. I am so, so sorry! You should have stuck with me though. That was the plan!"

"Yeah, well about that..."

"No, Jenny, please, we weren't a part of anything bad. I can explain everything if you let me."

I didn't really want to hear it.

"Look, it's been quite an eventful night and I just want to drive home with some calming music for a couple of hours and crash on my own comfortable bed, okay?"

I could see that Annie respected my wishes.

"Okay, I do understand, but perhaps we could swap phone numbers? It would be fab to keep in touch. I think you're an awesome person. I don't have any female friends. If you come down to the beach again then we should hang out, just you and I."

I was surprised to hear the offer, but didn't really want the hassle of any more crazy events.

She looked at me with soft eyes.

"Please?"

"Ah, what the heck, let me just get into my car first."

Ah shit! I just realised my car keys and clothes were by the table near the shed where we quickly got ready.

Annie held my key out to me. With a mixed sense of shock and relief, I grabbed it swiftly from the palm of her hand.

"I hoped you would find your way back. It was my only hope, so I picked your bits up and brought them up here. Your clothes are in the car."

Then I realised two things! One was that she wasn't going to steal my car! The second was that she assumed I wouldn't need 'search and rescue' out hunting for me. I could have died!

"Oh, well that was good thinking I'd say, but what if I hadn't made it to the car tonight?"

"Well, I guess I would have had a tonne of us out looking for you."

I couldn't help but think it was a big risk, simply hoping I'd make it back to the car, along with the cheek of helping herself to my items.

I just wanted to head home now.

Thankfully, I hid my purse and phone under the driver's seat.

I felt so relieved to feel them as I reached in.

Annie continued to talk whilst I fumbled around, checking everything was in its place. She didn't seem to mind me judging her by inspecting everything! I wasn't really paying attention to what she was saying, until I pulled my head back out of the door.

I caught the end of her sentence... *Mumbled voice,* "...You know?"

I didn't know what sentence she had just finished.

"Sorry, I missed what you said."

Annie didn't seem to be taken off trail by my request for the repeated words.

"I was just saying that perhaps we could surf together sometimes and have girlie chats. I miss all of that with hanging around men, you know?"

It was said as if she'd practiced it a few times, with the same ending of the sentence.

"Well, I guess we could surf together when I fancy coming down here."

"I'll make it worth your while for the travel. I can give you lessons and treat you to lunch."

It seemed a very kind offer, but I wasn't sure if she was still playing a game to draw me into the group for some reason.

I thought it would be easier to play the same game just to gain my departure.

"Okay, well, that's a nice idea. Maybe if you give me your mobile number, I'll store it in my phone and get in touch when I know I'm due to come down."

I poised my fingers over the phone, ready to take her contact details.

"Cool!"

She swiftly gave me her number and gave me a big hug before waving me off.

The relief I felt when driving off was huge! In some ways I found it very enlightening and exciting with my strange abilities, but in other ways I'm finding that it's drawing some crazy madness my way!

During the drive home I decided to play really loud music just to blast off the stress I had encountered. The calming music didn't happen at all! Thoughts were flying around my head like wildfire. This was like living half of the" Superman" life Sue was suggesting.

Although it's naughty, I couldn't help wonder if stealing from boats could be an easy money-maker using my abilities!
I thought on and decided that my morals were too strong to be the Supervillain! Despite that, my job comes naturally to me, as I'm really good with figures and management.
The drive made me think about how my new abilities would impact my life. I needed to make them a positive advantage, but to keep them out of sight to avoid being a science experiment. I know it was a consideration once however out of desperation.
Perhaps I could be **Jenny** by day and "**Jelly**" by night! In fact I decided to call my alternate-self **Jelly**. It made it fun. I did seem to become a bit rubbery in the arm flap and webbed areas! In fact, I haven't yet inspected my entire self when this alteration has occurred. I also wasn't sure if there were further changes that I wasn't aware of. So far I know I can adapt to water in very strange ways yet can also run swiftly and smoothly on the sand of a beach!

I was supposed to be a boring office worker! Perhaps this was some kind of destiny! A lot of thoughts went flying around my head for the entire journey home.

Despite the two hours of driving, I didn't expect it to go so swiftly, but then I was soaked in my own thoughts. A gift for the long journey really!

Before I knew it, I was pulling up onto my driveway, pulling a fresh surfboard and bag of new goodies out of my car.

I must have made a slight noise, as I noticed the curtain moving up in Patrick's bedroom. He was obviously peering out to see what was going on. It was certainly out of the ordinary for any unusual noises to occur in our neighbourhood, so it was understandable. I wanted to apologise, but that would mean disturbing him further. There would be other opportunities.

It wasn't too late considering the circumstances of the day and evening! I managed to get into bed by half past one in the morning. In my eyes that wasn't too bad, as at least I had a lot of the night to have a great sleep with.

When I *did* drift off, I had another very strange dream.

I was stood in a large, white room. The white was so pristine that it hurt my eyes a little bit. A kind man walked over to inspect my eyes. He confirmed that all was well with me and I felt relieved. After he walked away I looked in a very metallic mirror, almost as bright as the white shimmery walls that surrounded me. The mirror showed my eyes to have pupils like goats! My pupils were horizontal and my normal eye colour was almost orange! I played with my eyelids and they felt large and like rubber or something mouldable. My nose had moved flat onto my face, only leaving the nostrils in place. They looked as if they had flaps around them too! I looked in the mirror and breathed out heavy to watch my nostrils. The flaps flapped! So weird! I looked at my eyes and they were so freaky in their goat-like appearance.

I didn't feel uncomfortable in my dream, but wondered if I *should* have been, as another man came up from behind me and placed a material bag over my head. He said something in a language I didn't understand. I knew I could breathe through this material, but this wasn't exactly how I chose to be treated in *my* dream. I shouted through the material.

"I want respect!"

The man pushed me gently into a direction I knew I had been in before, but I resisted.

"I said I want respect!"

With that, I woke with a sweat in bed, still shouting that I wanted respect! I shouted it a couple of times into the darkness before I realised I was awake in my own bed.

It was early in the morning, but felt wide awake and ready to rise for the day. I knew I could nap if necessary with being on holiday.

The days merged into one another it seemed, with all of these weird occurrences falling on top of each other.

I felt as if I was actually in one long bizarre dream!

The odd dream of my eyes and nostrils came back to the forefront of my mind. It seemed very real and vivid.

I decided I couldn't waste my holiday focussing on analysing everything. I needed to accept that things were going to be different from now on. Somehow I accepted that there weren't going to be any definitive answers to all of this.

The morning went too swiftly. I didn't have time to think about how the day could possibly go. Perhaps that was good though, just for a change.

I was just about to prepare a lunch that would spoil me a little bit, when my phone made me jump out of my skin! Thankfully not literally, otherwise I would certainly freak out!

Jason!

Jason called me at a perfect time. I decided to answer since any communication right now would bring a comfort.

"Hi Jason," I'm certain my tone was really uplifting.

"Hey! Where have you been? I was hoping we could catch up soon. It seems forever since we last spoke."

I realised that I had been very distracted. After messing up accidentally with Jack, I didn't have men at the forefront of my mind. It was obviously a concern for me, that I wouldn't be able to share absolutely *everything* with them! I then chuckled under my breath about Sue's comment on my arm. I didn't want men to see an alien fanny in an odd place!

"I'm so sorry Jason. I've been quite active with some things and I just got carried away."

"Oh, it's okay. I get that we shouldn't rush into seeing each other too much. I just wondered if you fancied a lunch. I'm taking the rest of the day off to fix a few things, but thought you may still have some free time to have a meal with me."

"You know what? I really would like that. Whereabouts are you?"

"Well I'm just about to leave work, so I can meet you anywhere."

I must admit that it was really wonderful to hear Jason's voice. He timed it so well with how I was feeling. We arranged to meet at a coffee shop in a shopping centre near his work place. That way I could selfishly shop afterwards when he goes off to fix things! He told me that he has a couple of motorbikes that he likes to work on from time-to-time.

When we met, he arrived on one of his motorbikes, perhaps to impress me with his leathers! When I thought about it, his lunch may not have been a spontaneous idea.

At least he wanted to impress me. I daren't try to impress him at the moment!

We had a fantastic conversation about the bike hobby that I didn't know about before today. He told me of some travels he took part in that were quite extreme! Long distance journeys across countries, with minimal items. He didn't seem the type. To me he seemed someone who needed to keep his appearance very sharp! I initially felt I would need to be a high-maintenance lady to keep up with his good looks. The more I grew to know him, the less materialistic he seemed. I was impressed! He also wasn't

in such a rush to get me into bed. Obviously at this point in time I
was grateful for that, as I wasn't quite in tune with my new
abilities. I didn't want to ruin things the same way I did with Jack!
Jason seemed worth waiting for.

Our food and drink ended and we were too full to consume any
more. Naturally, our conversation came to a point where we
needed to change the scene.
He noticed the same, so we walked to his motorbike. I was
looking forward to my selfish shopping.
Jason was obviously feeling braver, as he reached over to grab
behind my neck, reeling me in for a passionate kiss. It felt
wonderful. His lips worked perfectly with mine. I relaxed into it
and enjoyed the feelings it prompted. At the same time I was
aware of my body, feeling for any weird changes. Thankfully all
was still and normal. Perhaps it was just about keeping calm. He
gently moved away and placed his motorcycle helmet on, reaching
his leg over the large leather seat. His kiss was a tease!
He started his engine and gave a lovely wink, before riding off like
some kind of movie hero.
Wow! I felt a bit jelly-like after that.

I was a bit distracted for a moment, so I stood there watching
other cars and bikes moving around before heading to the shops.
Jason was good at pulling the lady in! I knew his tactics were trust
building methods, but his kissing skills were enough to gauge his
level of passion.
I needed to move on from this spot now!

My mood was soon into shopping and I treated myself to a couple of clothing items. The novelty and good feeling of buying things was soon going to wear off, so I needed to think about my next plan. I still needed to enjoy my holiday and calculate what was needed to fulfil my life. It was important for me to remember that feeling I had at work before I decided to have time to reflect on things.

I questioned myself whilst shopping.

What was it I needed in my life?
What was I missing?

I had read a lot of books and watched plenty of movies about the importance of love in our lives. Finding someone to share my life with would be a good start, but I couldn't force something like that. I contemplated getting a dog, but the thought of my strange mutations may frighten the living daylights out of the poor thing!

I know I certainly needed things to calm down slightly after all of the crazy events. The craving for fun was still there however. I just didn't want to be dangerous about it!

Chapter Five

Karen, Claire and Kerry were sat on my sofa, chatting away over a glass of wine. This time was going to be different. We needed to talk and relax on this weekend day.

Since our mad drinking session it was decided that we would meet up more often.

I had some comfortable music on in the background and the lights were low. It was all to encourage relaxation and chatter.

Karen was always the one who instigated a lot of the conversation. She spent many years working in customer service roles, so she had a natural ability to find conversation in anything.

Claire was normally quite chilled out and more of a listener, seemingly choosing her words more cautiously. She would come out of her shell a lot more when quite intoxicated (of course!).

Kerry was a very easy going lady. She would do anything for anyone, given reason. I was in good company with these girls!

Everyone seemed happy to hear that Jason and I were getting on famously well and that I had dwindled dating numbers down to just one! I didn't explain that it was due to some super-mutating part of me ruining the first date!

We exchanged relationship frustrations and funny stories. I knew that having the ladies over would make me feel happier.

I enjoyed the feeling of us all being together, nattering.

We needed some nibbles, so I went into the kitchen to hunt for some nuts or crisps. Looking out of the window, I noticed a familiar car pulling up on my driveway.

Sue? ...Uninvited? Unusual!

I took a bowl of crisps in for the ladies and then walked back to the front door with the attempt to beat her to the doorbell.

Sure enough, Sue was only a couple of steps away from the door. Before I had chance to ask, she spoke.

"It's okay. It's just that I've been thinking. This is all okay. I just wanted to come over to give you some further moral support."

Guilt hit me hard! She was my greatest friend yet she hadn't been invited to this girlie chat! Perhaps I could quickly back track!

"Ah, actually, I've been doing okay. I invited some girls over for some company. In fact, now that you're here, I would love it if you would join us."

Sue looked past me to see the three figures sat chatting.

"Oh, well that's good. I'm happy to see you're coping."

"Did you want to come and join us?" I encouraged further.

"Well, I don't know anyone in your group. I would just feel weird barging in."

"You won't be barging in. I'd love it if you could join us in fact. You are my closest friend. It would be good for you to meet some of my other friends."

I was hoping she couldn't see the *guilt* in my thinking.

She was considering the invitation for a while.

"You know, I wouldn't mind, but not for long. I wasn't going to stop for hours. I just wanted to check you were okay."

I stood aside for her to enter.

It was fabulous to be creating my social circle at last. Somehow work caused my life to bypass me, but it was time to make up for it now.

Sue looked back at me as she entered my home, checking for information before settling in.

"Do they know?"

At first I didn't catch on to what she meant, as I was happy in this distraction.

"Oh, yes! I mean, no! They don't know."

Karen's head turned.

"They don't know what?"

I panicked!

"Oh, that... That Sue was going to come along and join us. I'm sorry! I forgot to say that she was going to stop by for a while."

Karen stood in politeness.

"Hi! You are obviously Sue."

Sue reached a hand out to Karen and gave a formal handshake. The other two stood and made things just as formal. It felt a little bit awkward, but I was hoping we could all bond somehow.

I needed to come up with some quick bonding ideas!

Sue settled into a single seat near me. She looked at me with an awkward smile and raised eyebrows.

"Oh sorry, did you want a drink?"

"If you have my usual, I wouldn't mind?"

Sue looked at the drink on the table but didn't seem keen. Mind you, she was driving.

I knew her well enough to automatically grab a glass of orange. It was her usual non-alcoholic drink.

We sat, looking at one another with polite smiles.

"Monopoly!" My single word came thrashing out.

"What?" Karen asked with a jokey tone.

"Let's all have a game. Maybe we could add an extra feature like a bet on the side."

"Ah, I'm no good at board games." Kerry wasn't exactly keen.

"A card game?" I was trying hard, "I have a poker set somewhere."

"Ah, go on then." Claire seemed keen for a bit of fun.

I knew Sue would be okay with a game, as she often suggested a game of Scrabble or Chess when she visited.

I could see that Sue was reading into my thoughts. She smiled with gratitude. We knew each other inside out.

A few moments in and a couple more large drinks of wine and we were all playing card games with fire in our hearts. I added "money chips" into the game for more excitement. Sue was always a natural at tactical games. She had accumulated the majority of chips as predicted. I wasn't doing too badly considering my wine levels were starting to get me a little merry!

This was the one habit I wasn't going to retain after my holiday! Drinking! I did make the most of it during our girl-time however.

I was beginning to regret the flow of wine at a later point. Upon awareness of everyone else, I could see that we were going against our plan to remain sober and in control!

Sue grew extremely comfortable with the other ladies, which was nice to see. Karen took to her extremely easily. Claire had the sensible character to blend well with Sue too. Kerry would get on with anyone anyway!

My lounge grew quite rowdy. The ladies seemed much louder and I'm sure I could include myself in that observation. Sue wasn't worried, but I did notice her glancing up at one of my clocks from time to time. I didn't want her to go, but I also didn't want her to feel uncomfortable in this group of drunken crazies! Sue and I have had our drunken moments together in the past, so we know each other at our worst. I just didn't want this to become one of them moments.

We did have quite a few bottles looking rather empty in the middle of my table. The crisps were topped up quite a few times. Kerry was really loosening up in her happiness. She was getting very loud. At one point she stood up to tidy her clothing, but started to move around the lounge with a hyper dance. It was funny to see. Everyone had a chuckle and encouraged her to sit down and play when it was her turn in the card games.
Claire started to dare everyone on the usual clothing removal when we lost a game, but I suggested it was no fun without a male presence. My reputation went downhill when she ran outside, asking for any males to come inside for a game of cards. Thankfully, anyone hearing her could see that she wasn't sober enough to pay attention to. The neighbourhood was usually too quiet to involve random men roaming the street.

Strangely however, there *was* a man of around thirty years of age that she somehow linked arms with and dragged into my home! I was about to tell him to head out, but Claire was so drunk that he appeared to be kind enough to be holding her up!

My front door was open and the girls wrenched the music volume up to club-style behaviours. Claire filled the young man with drink that wasn't even *hers* to give away, and began dancing provocatively in front of his body.

I noticed how Sue was beginning to let her hair down too without any drink at all. She laughed and joined in with Claire, slapping the poor man's bum with a firm hand. I could see that the man was partly nervous, but also hoping to get in on some action. This was getting a bit out of hand. Unless it was just me who wasn't loose enough to just have fun! There it was again. That *fun* word! It was always getting me into trouble!

Karen started to join in on the man attack, by placing the poker chips down the front of his jeans and asking him to pick random cards in order to fake magic tricks.

I decided just to drink more, to attempt to reach their intoxicated levels.
The man was eventually found to have the name of Justin.
He seemed to get into the feel of this invented, but unplanned party.

We were all flocking around Justin now, trying to tease him and encourage him to dance.

He grew confidence and politely moved my furniture into a position out of the way, exposing a nice space for us to bop around in. He appeared to be a kind and thoughtful man, who seemed to enjoy the attention once he settled into things.

I was certainly getting drunker now too, but I wasn't sure if Sue had been joining in on the drink, or just joining in on the atmosphere. She was acting very similar to Claire!

I was over-analysing, perhaps because this was happening in my own house!

Please leave everything in one piece!

I grabbed the nearest bottle and took many more gulps. I wondered what colour my vomit was going to be after all of this! A thought I needed to eradicate from my mind!

Another visitor appeared to be joining in. The open door invited the lovely Patrick from next door!

I can remember all of us ladies pouncing on him, encouraging him to join in, but he was trying to request a reduction in music volume. He gently waded through us to get to the speaker, but he couldn't figure out the system. I remembered a very insulting laugh coming from my mouth, which brought me to giggling tears. Patrick was definitely not very happy about our disruption to his normal life. He walked over to me with firm words.

"What the hell is going on with you lately? We've been neighbours for years and all of a sudden you're a drunken wreck, holding disruptive parties and inviting strange men in to your home." He pointed to the young man who was now too drunk to care of insults.

Three ladies were holding onto Justin from all directions, enjoying provocative dancing.

I knew I was slurring badly when I tried to tell Patrick that I was just having a bit of fun and that he should just join in. I tried to dance provocatively in close proximity to him, but he pushed me away gently and shook his head.

"Just turn the volume down on this speaker. Please!"

For a moment of slight soberness, I noticed deep pain in Patrick's eyes.

"Okay Patrick. I'm really sorry."

I reached over to the camouflaged buttons and reduced the volume. It was connected to my phone, so I also needed to reduce the volume on that.

"Cunning," Patrick seemed to think that the speaker technology was a ploy against him in itself!

"I'm s...s...sorry Paddy."

"I'll speak to you when you're sober young lady."

I couldn't believe he spoke to me like some child. He walked out unhappy, but obviously satisfied with the volume reduction. I knew an apology would come from me in good time, but at this moment, we were having a ball.

I didn't even think about how this all came to such a high-energy party. It just seemed to happen naturally.

Sue seemed slightly tipsy, so I knew she wouldn't be going home until the morning. I didn't see her crafty alcohol drinking, but I did suspect it was happening due to her behaviour.

A slight concern over how everyone was going to be after all of this came to mind.

Sue asked me for my phone. I didn't even ask why as I reached for it and handed it over.

She gained some selfies and took some videos of us dancing. At the time I felt so invincible, jumping around and slapping people on the heads. I have no idea what the slapping was about, but my excitement was almost uncontrollable. The thought of my strange body enhances were a slight worry, but I did keep looking at my arm and hands and they looked perfectly normal.

We danced and danced and rolled around on my sofa with funny ideas.

I vaguely remember Justin taking turns to snog each one of us and rating us out of ten. He somehow managed to locate a large felt-tip pen and writing pad. We were all holding our breath with the scores as if our lives depended on it, but then laughed care-free with more wine flowing into us.

The following morning I shouldn't have been surprised at the carnage.

I was on my bed, trying to find my hair with my fingers, opening my eyes gradually to a stuffy head. There were another two bodies lying on my bed in funny positions. The unrecognisable Justin was comfortably huddling into Karen. I noticed one of Karen's arms were holding onto one of my legs. Somehow there was only vague recollection of the final hour of our event! I remember Karen declaring the need for company when going to sleep. Justin kindly offered his cuddles to help her. Of course there was the risk of more occurring on my own bed! Upon my scan over the bed, I noticed everyone was still fully clothed! Huge relief filled me.

I managed to crawl gently onto the ground and find my way to the bathroom. I wanted to beat the rest of them to it. I didn't bother to inspect the rest of the house until I threw myself together. The mirror didn't demonstrate a heavy party. This was a pleasant surprise since this so-called party *did* start early in the day and work late into the night. Perhaps I danced a lot of the alcohol out of my system. I always needed to calculate reasons. It seemed I was a natural analyst. Others were able to let loose and simply "be".

I worked through my hair and refreshed myself to an improved state. The same clothes would remain on to avoid waking anyone.

I walked into the lounge to find the other ladies comfortably sleeping on the sofa and chairs. Kerry was tucked into a tight ball on one of the chairs, covered with her jacket. I thought she actually looked quite sweet, like a little animal.

Patrick's face came to mind when I walked into the kitchen to grab a stimulating drink of coffee.

The horrible thought of facing my reality once all of my post-party friends had departed went repeatedly around my head. There's always the baseline life we need to return to. Parties were always going to be temporary.

Everyone gradually rose from their heavy pits. Sue seemed worst hit by the drink. I felt like the nurse and waitress despite feeling a bit fragile myself.

Ah the woes of being the hostess!

I heard Karen and Justin talking in my bedroom quite vocally. It wasn't an argument, but a healthy discussion that neither of us could quite make out. It could be the predicted "I'm a taken woman, but thanks for the company last night", kind of conversation.

At one point everyone sat around in my newly, corrected arrangement of the lounge, drinking coffee and talking nicely. It felt lovely and relaxed, like a little family.

Justin was an instant hit in friendship. I could tell that everyone felt comfortable with him.

During the conversation he told us a little about himself. Something we should have done prior to the drunken bonding. He was a spring chicken compared to us, yet so mature in his conversation.

Sue was keen to get home after our coffee and chat, which was understandable, given that she was only intending on a brief stay! Each person left gradually, one by one, once Sue had departed.

When the house was empty of people, I quickly cleaned up and changed my bedsheets. A shower came, followed by a re-dress with the intention to head over to Patrick's.

The brief walk to Patrick's seemed a street-length worth! I didn't want to face my "bad behaviour" apology, but it was necessary. Patrick answered the door promptly and invited me in. I smelt a strong aroma of pizza coming from the kitchen, which seemed to produce excessive saliva in my mouth. The craving for it was immense!
Patrick invited me to his lounge for a gentle conversation. He called for his wife to bring some soft drinks for comfort. I felt spoilt, yet not worthy. He was so kind and wonderful, considering my disrespectful and thoughtless disruption to his household.
We sat comfortably on his very expensive looking sofa. The style of his house demonstrated his Italian heritage. I always found it amazing how people from different traditions could make a bare home look so wonderfully cultured.

"So, Jenny, I noticed you have changed your lifestyle lately. I don't judge or try to control anyone obviously, but it is just a concern."

I took a sip of orange juice that his wife kindly provided. It felt so smooth on my mouth. It felt like a combination of luscious fruit. The taste distracted me in a wonderful way.

"Tasty fruit?"

Patrick commented on the drink before I could. He obviously pleased his customers in the same way in his restaurants.

"Only the best food and drink is used in this home."

"I can taste that! I can even see that in your décor standards."

"Why thank you Ma'am."

"Oh, please remember I prefer to be referred to as Jenny."

"Oh, it is force of habit. So, Jenny, I am concerned for your welfare. I have seen some unusual occurrences with you lately and wondered if you need some help in any way. I have known you here for years, but seen more strangeness in the last week or two."

It hit me that Patrick was very observant. He continued...

"Jenny, are you in any kind of trouble? We can help you, you know?"

He was such a kind man. I couldn't believe *how* kind!

"We know that you must be quite vulnerable living in that house all on your own. We have only ever seen a parent or random friend visit you normally. Now, I know we can have our flare-ups in life, but I'm sure we know your behaviours enough to recognise a change in circumstance. We are just concerned."

His English was much better than his initial impression.

I placed my drink on a small metallic table near me to prepare an explanation. Obviously I wasn't going to tell him that I am a secret "Jelly woman!"

"Well, Patrick you are very observant and instinctive and also unusually kind."

He smiled, inviting his wife into the room with a movement of his hand. I continued on, wondering why two of them needed to hear any explanation I may have. I dropped my barriers however and opened up best I could.

"Well, I was getting a bit fed-up with work one day and decided I needed to live a little. I don't know if I'm reaching a certain age, or if I just had some kind of wake-up call, but I needed some time to let my hair down. Unfortunately, I'm not too familiar with what happens when we put ourselves out there a bit more than usual. I've had some unfortunate occurrences and involvement in things I didn't choose to be involved with."

Patrick didn't look surprised.

"Oh, I see. Are you in any kind of trouble though? I don't want to see you struggling in any bad situation. It's best to knock things on the head as soon as possible."

I wondered what Patrick was assuming. He could see my confusion, so he elaborated for me.

"Well, you aren't involved in anything unlawful, or anything harmful to yourself are you? Nothing that could create crime or danger? You don't have substances or pending situations?"

I wondered for a moment if Patrick was involved in some kind of undercover operation, the way he spoke to me with such interrogation. Then I realised his concerns for the neighbourhood. His mind could be focussed on the attraction of crime to the area.

"Oh Patrick, I'm not involved in any gangster stuff, or drug situation. You can be assured that every bit of fun I've been involved in has ended just as soon as it had begun. I'm not tangled up in anything."

I noticed Patrick and his wife dropping their heads in relief.

My next question should have been predictable to them.

"So, what the heck did you think I was involved in?"

"Oh, nothing specific, we were just worried about you so much. We couldn't explain the events we were seeing from our windows or the noises flying through the neighbourhood."

I still couldn't believe how good his English was. Our first proper chat over coffee during my car defacing event, gave me the impression he was looking hard to put the sentences together. Either way he was demonstrating kindness and wisdom. It was wonderful to know that my neighbour was actually watching over me!

We sat with general chat for absolutely ages. We moved to their perfectly polished dining table, where we ate the most amazing pizza. I could see how they made their money from the food business. Their cooking talents were amazing!

It was enjoyable to have intellectual conversation without the need to find fun with crazy amounts of alcohol or risky situations. I realised with this that I needed to find balance in life again.

I decided to take some time out for the next few days and just to see the holiday break out with calm and safety. I not only owed it to my neighbours, but to myself to have the rest and recuperation.

I also needed to rebuild my confidence levels in life after all of the madness.

Chapter Six

I was preparing my appearance in the bathroom, feeling nervous about returning to work.
Looking very sharp with my suit and make-up on, I felt ready to leave the house.

I climbed into my courtesy car, reminding myself of the need to look into the completed insurance claim. This car was a lovely replacement for now, but I wanted my own choice of vehicle again. I felt so spoilt thinking that way. This holiday brought on so many humbling events that materials didn't seem important to me.

I noticed Patrick stood at the front of his house.
It looked as if he was expecting my reverse from the driveway, as he waved happily to see me off.

Upon reflection of my holiday, I realised I had built stronger friendships and found a sweet person to date. What more could a holiday bring? I felt I had achieved many things that I would never have expected.

Walking into the reception, the atmosphere felt cold and too clinical. We needed life and personality to fill the void. Perhaps this was what I was noticing about work before the holiday idea.

The receptionist said good morning in a very vibrant manner, but when I tried to make conversation with her, she seemed to struggle with any continuity. Perhaps she had programmed herself so much with the "good morning" message that she wasn't sure what would be said beyond that. She appeared to work hard on something on her monitor. I hoped that it was simply *that* distraction.

The open plan area was filled with busy heads, soaked into their screens. If only we could all see ourselves from the "looking in" view, just simply staring at our screens. If the screens weren't there, we would be staring into space.
I don't know why I was thinking this way. Life had given me so many different themes for a couple of weeks.

I walked into my office. Everything looked exactly the same. Nothing appeared to be waiting for me.
James spotted me and kindly walked over to give me a welcoming hand shake.
"Welcome back. Did you get everything you needed from your break? Are you ready to get back to things now?"

I felt a little relieved with the welcome, since it felt so cold upon the approach. It wasn't a great feeling walking through a robotic office space, with no greeting.

James saved the day. I would probably have wanted to go straight back home otherwise.

"Hi boss. It's good to be back."

What a lie!

"It's good to have you back Jenny. We need your expertise on a few matters. I'll come to your office in a short while to update you."

"Ah thanks James."

He gave me a smile. I also noticed him kindly request for a coffee to be delivered to my office. It was an unnecessary step to please me, but it certainly helped me emotionally.

My office felt so bland now. I sat to get things going, shuffling some old sheets of figures about.

A leaflet sat on the side. These things usually ended up in my recycling bin, but today I had a different mind.

"Paragliding fun!
2 for 1 deal on Sundays!"

I could feel myself heading for trouble just with the thought of it. I smiled to myself with the prospect.

My mobile phone flashed the announcement of a text from Jason. It was just prompting me to get in touch to arrange another date.

At this moment I wasn't really interested in rushing straight into work. I spent a few minutes sending messages back and forth, with one predictively suggesting the paragliding. He didn't seem to hold back on the idea of an adventure. His message seemed very keen to give it a go.

This prompted me to work with a better attitude. There was something and someone to look forward to. I decided this was just simply a money-maker and nothing else. No emotions, just simply a place to earn and then head home. That's how everyone else seemed to treat it in here.

Kathy, a lovely lady from our office canteen came to offer me the prepared cup of coffee that James had requested. I felt spoilt and guilty at the same time.

"Here you go Jenny. Did you have a nice holiday? Rumour has it that you were really needing it!"

Oh great, so rumours were obviously flying around too!

"Oh Kath, I just wanted a holiday. There was nothing else to it. You can set the rumour straight if you like."

"Oh sorry my love, people were just genuinely concerned for you."

"Ah, I'm sorry Kath. I didn't mean to sound rude. Thank you for the coffee."

"It's a pleasure ma' dear. Listen, I don't know if anyone has said, but we are having a quiz evening after work today. Some of the lads are definitely hanging around for it."

I chuckled, recalling our frequent conversations about my single life.

"Oh Kath, please don't say anything, but I am dating someone at the moment. Mind you, I might be tempted with some of the office boys if the quiz brings some relaxed attitudes."

"Ah Jenny, I'm so happy for you. I really hope this chap looks after you and it builds to something wonderful."

"Thanks!"

"I think Des is meant to be coming later though. You can't deny your little eyes on him over the years."

Des was someone way out of my league, but I couldn't help having a nice stare at him every now and then. He was the type you could visualise in a Hollywood movie... Just the perfect chiselled facial and bodily features. He certainly looked after himself - a picture of perfection.

"Ah, well only if you can get us on the same table!"

"I could work on that for you love." She gave a twinkly smile. We both chuckled and continued on about our ways.

After a few hours I felt very much at home, working through figures, knowing this was my skill for life. It didn't hurt to settle back into normal life, keeping a smooth flow of routine for distraction and a vital income.

As the day moved on, I did have a few queries from people visiting the office, asking me how my break was. It did feel a little bit more sociable as the hours ticked by. My first impression of returning was perhaps a little harsh. It just felt so cold and dull initially.

I kept the same routine daily throughout the weeks. At first I found it hard to comply to, as my freedom felt diminished. The odd Yoga class returned, but with more to talk about with the ladies. We all chuckled intensely over the fun we had. Justin decided to join our Yoga group, adding to the humour! I had a few more innocent dates with Jason, mostly over a coffee or meal.

Life felt good. The "mutations" didn't bother me at this point in time. My arm, feet and hands converted every time I had a shower, but it didn't matter, as it was a private moment anyway. It took adjustment, but over time I realised it only had place when water was involved. Thankfully, rain didn't set anything off, perhaps because the droplets weren't enough to have to swim or bathe in!

As the summer kicked in with hotter days I started craving the sea again. I didn't think it would be possible to head back to the same seafront with risk of bumping into the crowd of thieves. I also had no true intention of keeping in touch with Annie, although guilt played a part there. They did feel comfortable to be with at the time. It did sadden me to think I couldn't trust them despite the majority of them seeming so kind, inviting and friendly.

There were plenty of beaches, but that particular beach was a favourite of mine.
After a lot of contemplation, I decided to say "stuff it!" I was just as entitled to go to the same beach! If I bumped into the crowd then I don't have to answer to them! If they cause me any issues,

then I would just bring on my abilities and use my strength to swim away! I'm not sure why I was creating my defence plans, already predicting a negative situation when it may not even happen!

I called Jason to see if he fancied a weekend of surfing and swimming. He seemed a little bit nervous about an entire weekend, so we selected a full Sunday, providing the weather was reasonable enough. It was predicted to be just as hot and sunny as it had been recently.

We were already on our day trip! I wanted to drive, to make the most of the free mileage on the courtesy car. I had the surfboard in the back and a few usual beach items, including the fun of a prepared picnic. This seemed to be a level of fun that I was comfortable with.

Jason, on the other hand was teasing me so many times with passionate kisses and fondling moments, but we still hadn't approached the sex! I wondered if he was shy, or if he had some kind of build-up tactic that fed his fantasies. I knew I couldn't bring the subject up just yet, as it could crumble his plans. Several weeks had already passed however, so I was trying to analyse it. I know I shouldn't... And I know sex shouldn't be the total aim.

As I drove, I wanted to explain some of my concerns about going to the same beach I had issues with. I broached the subject casually.

"So have you ever been to this beach?"

"Oh yes, I just haven't spent much time at that one. I normally head further east because there's a bit more entertainment further along."

"Oh, I didn't realise. What kind of entertainment?"

"You'll think I'm sad, but sometimes I go down with my mates to go on the arcade machines and then grab a beer with fish and chips afterwards. The biggest money maker from the arcade games would be the person paying out for the beers and grub."

I didn't see much wrong with that. The beach style of entertainment and food was generally that for many!

"That's fair enough! I've had the odd dabble."

"Dabble? It's just a laugh. We had great times as young lads, but it doesn't happen often these days. In fact some summers bring us a reunion time just to re-live the moments, although now that we earn a proper living, we can get even more carried away with the beers."

He laughed pretty hard with his obvious recalling of memories.

I liked that though. He was showing his "bloke" character which I needed to see a bit more of for some reason.

"I'd love to see that as a fly on the wall."

We chuckled for a few moments as he recalled a few stories.

I wanted to get back to my aim of the subject.

"This beach is a little weird for me. When I was teaching myself to surf, there was this kind bunch of surfers who invited me to a barbeque party thing. They got me surfing in the night for a bit."

"Wow, that's cool. You're in with some surfers!"

"Yeah, kind of, it's just that I think they're the wrong kind of crowd. I think they're into some dodgy stuff, so I decided to keep away from them."

"Eek, so we're going to a beach of surfers who may have a disliking to you?"

"Ah, it's not as bad as it sounds. You see, there's a lady called Annie who's really keen to have me surf with her. I told her I'd keep in touch, but I didn't. I told her I'd let her know when I'm visiting so we can hook up."

"Oh, so it's cool with you guys? I'd love to hang out with surfers."

"Well, I haven't been in touch since and time has passed. I'm also about to get there without any care for telling her I'm visiting."

"Oh well. It doesn't matter if you think about it. You're taking me. Things have changed since. You're hooked up with someone."

I smiled at the idea of him stating that we were "hooked up."

"I guess you're right there. I'm in a different set of circumstances this time around." I smiled, "I guess I'm just a bit nervous about them bumping into me."

"Well, what could they possibly do if they do recognise you?"

It was a good question. I wasn't sure if I was just being stupidly paranoid.

"That's true. I think we would just be doing the best thing if we pick a more private sea patch, if you know what I'm getting at?"

"Yeah, you just don't want to create any scenes. Let's just focus on enjoying the day."

He was right. I didn't know why I was focussing on that so much. I think I wanted to explain any weird behaviour.

"Let's put some happy music on hey?" I decided that would lift the fun spirits back up!

The rest of the journey involved singing and excitement about trying the surfing and swimming on such a beautiful day.

It wasn't long before we were setting up camp on a slightly quieter selection of sand. The place was quite busy, bringing me comforts of blending into crowds.

Our towels were in perfect position and our bodies were exposed to the sun. Jason was wearing a perfect short-style pair of trunks and I'd hoped I'd picked the best bikini for his eyes. I wasn't attempting to provoke anything sexual at this time. I just wanted him to be proud of me amongst the many other attractive ladies. I knew he wasn't worried about image too much, but I didn't want him to be repelled by me! Perhaps I was overthinking again!

I noticed Jason was wearing the same water sport type shoes. He didn't seem to want to take them off for freedom of his feet. I couldn't help but comment.

"Don't you want to feel the sand between your toes?"

He looked as if I had sworn in his face! I instantly apologised without logical reasoning.

"I'm sorry. Please do as you wish. Be comfortable."

I guess I didn't know him inside out just yet.

He looked down and looked as if he wanted to confess a few things.

"No, *I'm* sorry. I should explain something to you. I just hoped I could get away with it."

I worried now, wondering what he was about to confess!

"You see, I had an accident some years ago, so I prefer to keep things covered up as it kind of freaks people out if they spot it."

By the words "spot it", it didn't sound like a very conspicuous thing, but it was obviously a big deal to him.

He slowly removed one of the shoes, looking very nervous.

As the shoe exposed his foot, it revealed to me that all of his toes were missing!

"It's just one foot." He explained as if he was trying to justify a crime or something.

It made me think about my mutation weirdness. He had nothing to worry about if he compared himself to me!

"Oh jeepers Jason! I'm not going to treat you any differently for that! It's not your bits and pieces I'm interested in. You're a perfect ten to me!"

He grinned widely with a surprised heightened set of eyebrows. "This doesn't bother you?"

"Of course not! What kind of woman do you think I am?"

He grinned with a cheeky set of eyes, obviously about to say something humorous. "Well then, I hope you won't be disappointed when I confess to this then. " He began to open his shorts up to reveal some of his pubic hair. "I'm only kidding!"

He chuckled with great humour for a few moments.

"You know, you're great Jen. Many ladies have left me simply over my imperfection, as if they just couldn't get past it with their minds."

"Jee, well I'm so glad we met. None of us are perfect."

"So, tell me what your imperfections are then. You don't seem to have any identifying flaws."

"We all have flaws Jase."

I realised we were starting to comfortably abbreviate our names. It was always a great sign.

"I guess you'll have to wait and see. I have everything in the right places, but it depends on the eye that's looking."

"Well, that's a true comment. You seem perfect to me."

He always seemed to say the right things. I just hoped he meant it.

Jason seemed happier than he'd ever been since we met. He admitted he wasn't comfortable about having a full weekend away just in case I didn't approve of his foot! My new concerns were that we were growing closer emotionally. That wouldn't normally be an issue, but for obvious reasons I had a heck of a lot more to confess. The mutual thing between us was that neither of us could help our physical attributes. Mine would take a heck of a lot more of an explanation, since I couldn't even give one for myself!

I suddenly wished for the explanations for what my body was doing or going through. I couldn't blame any hormonal change that's for sure! I'm certain there wouldn't be anyone else who could make such comparisons!

The next challenge would be getting into the sea without a wetsuit! I did bring a large elbow support, in order to cover the arm "gill", but I didn't have the ability to cover my hands and feet without looking completely bonkers! In most surfing cases, it was just the arm that converted, so I needed to hope that this would be the case for today!

I grabbed the surfboard and suggested some play in the water. Jason was advising that he just stuck to the body boarding to avoid getting his feet out. I didn't realise he had a concern about everyone else noticing his foot. This shouldn't have surprised me. I was being the dishonest one with my arm support now!

We had a mix of surfing and bodyboarding between us. It was fantastic fun and no beginner's injuries were at play. Jason decided to have a swim for quite a while so that I could practice the surfing for longer. I wanted him to have equal time, but he was having great fun just the same. It was such a bonding day. We cared about each other's wellbeing and discovered we were really big beach lovers.

We had a few unexpected belly laughs. I had lost my bikini parts a few times with epic falls into the water. He had a huge wave crash into him when he appeared to be stood, posing.

So many silly little things made us laugh uncontrollably. We both cuddled up on the towels with salt water dripping from us, laughing and encouraging each other to head back in for more water fun.

Jason declared that he may ache on the Monday for overdoing the swimming when he wasn't used to exercising for an entire day. His body looked as if he exercised every minute of the day however. I loved his washboard abdominals and the shape of his well-cut pectorals. Anyone would get the impression of him being an extremely active person!
In fact we complimented one another on our finely tuned shapes.

After our successful day on the beach, we drove halfway home to find a nice looking public house for food.
Our conversation was fulfilling and equal. I felt this could be the beginning of a lifetime relationship. We were both excited to be with one another. At this point I had a completely different perception of having sex with Jason! With him being such a lovely person, I realised it wasn't the be-all-and-end-all. I never did see relationships as something purely focussed on sex, but since we both have young and fit bodies it seemed something that becomes part of the process early on. I realised I may have been existing in a generalised thought-system. Jason was worth more than just the sharing of bodily fluids!
It grew late and I knew we needed to face the fact of getting home. I could tell we would be heading straight to our own homes, with early work plans the next day. It was fine. The day brought much joy.

The week brought continuity of routine again. Jason and I had booked the Paragliding event, which meant another day of fun and adventure together. At least I could experience fun again, but with someone else to share it with. There were hopes that the fun would literally remain that way – fun! I didn't want any unfortunate incidents to be incorporated! Fun was always meant to be fun!

During the week I didn't get the opportunity to spend time with Jason, but this time we did agree to a full weekend away!

Yoga lessons were part of the routine, and Justin still came along to receive his regular flirtation. Claire seemed to grow close to him in a more mature way. I could see that there were temptations, but Claire stuck to her loyalties at home. We all had a few laughs every time however. Our group sessions were certainly lively these days! Everyone was so loyal to the sessions, knowing they'd have their uplifting chuckles with the exercise.

It was the end of the working day of Friday, and the week had absolutely flown by! Sue was due to come over for more of a private catch-up. I prepared some chocolatey nibbles for us, but decided not to offer any wine this time!

Sue arrived and walked in joyfully. She could see that I was comfortable with my life situation which brought her much contentment in return. We nibbled and nattered over our favourite movie. It was a nice girly evening. The conversation about my mysterious abilities began to build at the predictable time of the movie.

"So, have you discovered anything else about yourself lately? Or is it calm on the green fanny front?"

"Ha-Ha! Only you could say things like that."

She laughed at my response through a mouthful of chocolate.

"Well, all I know is that I have the traits of some kind of Amphibian when I get into water. I'm perfectly normal otherwise."

"Did you decide to get yourself checked out somehow? Any science study agreement?"

"Ha! I just thought I would leave it and accept it. My life is pretty happy at the moment. If it keeps as settled as it is, then I've got nothing to worry about."

"So do you have flipper feet too?"

Only Sue could be so direct with me. We were best-buddy level of familiarity.

"Similar! I can swim really fast and I feel really strong when I'm in the sea I noticed. I had an incident that forced me to swim away and it felt amazing!"

"So you are playing the superhero! It is some weird reality though isn't it? Do you need some kind of support do you think? I mean professional support? Just that I know after I noticed your green flaps, I felt like I needed some kind of therapy!"

"Gosh. What would you be like if you saw my normal skin flaps? Ha!"

"Well, I think I saw them once when Jemma gave us our first waxing session."

"Ha-Ha! Oh yes!" I recalled our very first attempt at that.

Waxing was new to us a few years ago, when we were fortunate enough to have a mutual Beauty Therapist friend.

It brought many painful laughs and a bit of girly time.

I realised I had lived a bit of a sheltered life up until now. People were probably sleeping about and living it up all of the time, while I was easing into some kind of balanced level of fun after a peak of madness. The only thing I'm sure others couldn't claim was the ability to adjust their body to do spectacular things! Well, the strange spectacular things that were happening to my body were just out of this world!

Sue ate an entire place of chocolate goodies, while I only had a small and gradual amount. I assumed that she was comfort eating as she certainly wouldn't have been hungry.

That same evening I had an email from my insurers to confirm that my claim was complete. This was a huge relief. I was able to spend a fund of the value of my car to treat myself to something new and fresh of my choosing. Shopping for something big like this would make me feel wonderful.

Sue was happy to hear this news too, as it brought new smiles to my face. We loved seeing one another doing well in life. To some we may seem spoilt, but we worked hard for everything we had. I visualised the amount of hours I must have clocked up in my career so far. The late nights to complete projects or to tidy up our end-of-year finances were long and tiresome. One thing I realised I had control of recently was the life and work balance. The holiday was a fantastic choice to have made. Everything following that allowed great and positive new changes.

Sue monitored my expressions as we flicked in and out of our movie that we'd seen between us umpteen times! She could see that I was vibrant in happiness. The new things in my life were meant to find me.

We enjoyed each other's company and found great calm and comfort in the present moment.

Saturday morning arrived swiftly. I woke to a very bright and sunny day. I packed a healthy bag of clothing, towelling, food and make-up items to prepare for my foresighted-positive weekend ahead. Jason and I were more comfortable about our insecurities and enjoyed the eye candy of one another. Our conversations were mentally stimulating and our passion was burning intensely. I wondered if Jason was feeling the pressure of sexual expectance. I had prepared my words to comfort him if he didn't feel ready. It was one subject we hadn't delved into! He certainly flirted and made enough advances to give me the impression that it would happen one day. I just wanted it to be right for both of us if it was going to happen. This only ever happened once before in my life, when I dated someone who didn't appear to feel comfortable about any love making. When he kissed me, it was enough for him to giggle intensely for a few minutes. I didn't know if it was because I was too funny, or if he was extremely nervous. In the end I discovered he preferred the company of men. Jason certainly didn't give me *that* impression. If I had suspected it for one second, then I would have encouraged him to be honest about his true desires. I was more concerned that he had some kind of underlying stigma over the approach. Either that or we had slipped into the *very* "friend zone" that made it difficult to move forward. Ah well, here I was overthinking again!

I didn't remember much about the bag-packing process, as my thoughts were focussed so much on how the weekend was going to pan out!
Relax!

Maybe *I* was the one with the sexual tension!

Jason came over to pick me up. I was happy for him to know where I lived now, and I didn't seem to worry about Patrick's assumptions when observing yet another man coming to my door! I suddenly had image awareness and felt proud to have such a great man walk up my driveway. It was nice to view him pacing up toward my front door. He was wearing really smart jeans and a comfortably fitted light opened shirt. It was very attractive, but not exactly beach wear. Upon thinking about it, we were settling into a hotel room first!

Ooh! This was exciting!

I opened the door to a passionate kiss and loving hug. It felt so wonderful. He picked up my bags and invited me into his car. He had a sporty red, convertible one that I didn't catch the make and model of, but it didn't matter. The roof was down and we were about to have a fun, free journey!

The hotel room was wonderful. Jason had ordered it and he obviously spent quite a bit of money on some added features! There were red and white petals on the bed spread, and someone had already set a welcoming, romantic radio station of gentle, encouraging tunes to fill the sound space. The bed covers looked intriguingly velvety. The colour features of the entire room were of red and whites, with the odd cream to blend the two very cleverly.

Just as I was about to give my words of mesmerisation, he lured me in gently for one of his amazing kisses.

I couldn't help but have an instant concern about my excitement after my last hotel room experience!

Jason could feel tension in my lips and asked if I was nervous. I admitted that I just wanted it to be so perfect. This was the encouragement to allow him to open up his feelings too!

He didn't want to rush anything and just wanted everything to be perfect for our first time.

My concerns were of my great strength kicking in again! I certainly didn't want to hurt *his* bits! Our first time had such a build-up, along with the money he'd spend on this room! – I just couldn't ruin it for either of us!

He removed my clothing and I melted into jelly with his comforting massage all over my body. I followed with the removal of his clothing. It was all very passionate and full of amazing foreplay! He grew to a time where he slipped the prepared condom on and began the sexual process of entrance!

I knew I was ready for him and allowed a smooth flow of action!

He kissed me hard and pushed hard into me. The action was perfect, up until he rushed into a fast rhythm and stopped suddenly. He dropped a lot of bodyweight onto my chest.

It was at that point that I realised the build-up had been way too long! He didn't last longer than a few seconds!

I felt slightly disappointed but sympathetic at the same time.

It wasn't until he collected his breath that he apologised.

"I'm so, so sorry. It wasn't meant to be like that. It was so hard not to."

"Ah don't you darn well worry. Let's rest and try again later. I did think our desires were drawn out, but we both had our worries."

"You're right. I had my worries about body image, but then when I knew you'd be fine with it, I've just been too excited about the whole thing!"

He rolled over onto his back, holding onto my hand.

It felt lovely despite the brief encounter!

It was a little bit quiet between us for a while. I noticed he was about to have a little kip, so I crept up from the bed to take a shower in private. It was the ultimate opportunity to check myself over for any strange occurrences, whilst cleaning up!

I noticed that everything was in perfect human tact, considering my excitement. It was shortly after drying off that Jason came into the bathroom, looking for a kiss. He apologised for falling asleep this time.

"I'm really sorry about that… and the sleep. Maybe it was the tension of it all and then the release."

"Stop your worrying. Let's sort out some beach time and leave the bed stuff for later, and even then there will be no pressure from me."

He smiled and hugged my naked body, making me feel like I needed another shower! I couldn't risk another one in his eye line!

We managed to make it to the beach. We walked along with our goods, trying to find a nice spot to rest on. Our humour built when we joked about the silly pressures of sex.

I suddenly felt a thud of panic fall into my feet when I noticed some familiar-faced surfers walking back up onto the shore towards us!

I dragged Jason into a different direction in panic. He nearly lost his footing and needed to re-juggle his feet in the deep sand. At that point I should have chuckled, but my full view was on avoiding the surfers.

"What the heck was that?" It was the first time Jason showed any disagreement.

"Ah shit! I'm really sorry... you know that group of surfers I was telling you about before?"

"Uh huh," Jason was obviously peeved about being dragged across the sand.

"Well, need I explain that I'm trying to escape their recognition of me?"

Jason looked over with a tight turn of his head, with his feet scuffling in the opposite direction.

"I was guessing!"

I looked over to notice Jason's expression of a frown and thin smile together.

"Ah, I'm so sorry! I didn't mean to drag you like that!"

"Well, let's call a truce, since I've also had to apologise today!"

I chuckled, seeing the funny side of it all.

The surfers were walking swiftly up the beach, not paying attention to any peripheral action. In fact they seemed to be rushing out of the water for some odd reason.

I stopped to watch in curiosity, noting the entire crowd of surfers walking or running swiftly up the beach and away from the water. I then looked out to sea to notice some kind of chaos between people. I noticed that same boat from before, floating in the distance. This boat appeared to have people scuffling all over it. Then there were smaller boats surrounding it and people jumping off and climbing on. It could have been mistaken for either a party or some kind of attack! I wanted to know more, so tried to focus in with my senses. At this point, my senses seemed a lot sharper! My hearing could pick up sounds from miles away! I attempted to tune-in to the boat noises and I could hear terror cries of help!

I looked at Jason.

"Can you hear that chaos over by that boat?"

He looked at me with concern and then followed his eyes to the same direction as mine.

"I can't tell from here." He confirmed that my senses were more enhanced!

Jason was disinterested in the event - understandably if all seemed normal to him.

I wanted to know what was happening, but didn't know how I could without getting all mixed up in the madness.

Shortly after the initial notice of chaos, I heard a lifeguard running in the distance! I mean, I literally heard his feet land on the sand. How could I hear that from this distance? I noticed the fit lifeguard running between the sunbathers. It seemed to me that they were trying to keep whatever it was under wraps, but it couldn't be clearer to me that something was going on.

I looked over at Jason and he seemed calm and unaware of everything around him. He was focussed on finding us a good spot on the sand. The chaos seemed to call me like some kind of radar signal. I couldn't ignore it! I don't know why it appeared to be calling me in!

Within the next few seconds, Jason found a lovely spot for our towels and items. I laid my towel out and made excuses to go out hunting for a toilet. He happily kissed me before I casually walked away.

When I knew I was out of sight, I ran into the sea. It was easy to run into the shallow parts, when usually I'd be fighting even the smallest wave. I felt strong and focussed. This strange "radar" signal was pulling me in. I jumped into the deeper water and felt something tingly about my back. As I swam under the water with my arm-gill crazily breathing for me, I reached back with one hand to feel some kind of blade sticking out of my spine! The only

association I had with it was that it could have been similar to a blade that would help me move faster through water. It didn't matter right now, as I was moving at super speed towards the boat, moving my limbs underwater like some mad alligator! I didn't know much about them however, other than what I noted on television. My eyes were comfortable in the salt water. Everything about me adapted to deep water swimming. Here was the "Jelly" version of me again!
Jelly coming to the rescue!

I grew close to the boat and noticed a rubber dingy and speedboat just on the outside of the boat. I didn't want to be noticed, so swam to the opposite side and kept under water. A rumbling ahead made me look up to notice a helicopter approaching the area too! I heard some voices telling some of the public to move back to the beach. Something crazy must be going on.
I swam up to the quiet side of the boat and drew my eyes up close to the smooth silver, slippery metal that I was planning to climb! It was amazing that I managed to use my sucker pads on my palms and soles of the feet in order to secretly climb up to the edge of the main internals of the boat. From the edge, I did my secret spying task, to observe the story. If anyone could see me from a bird's eye view, they would have seen a body "stuck" to the side of a boat.
I hoped that if I was caught I'd be unrecognisable. In my mind I visualised myself as a human-fish or alligator.

I couldn't see much occurring, but I knew something big was going on, whether I spotted it instantly or not.

A couple of people were encouraged to climb over the edge and into a dingy or speedboat on the other side. I recognised the jewellery on one of their arms and realised they were the two people who owned the boat! Their outlines were recognisable as the two bodies that were lying on the sunbeds whilst I was hunting for the surfer last time!

They'd been instructed to evacuate their own boat!

Someone looked very official, snooping around the boat with some kind of detecting tools.

I looked at myself, wondering how I was going to behave inconspicuously if I was going to climb into the main part of the boat. I looked down to notice that my hand seemed a different colour. My hand seemed to be more of a grey colour, blending into the silvery colour of the edge. I didn't understand that, but I didn't want to focus on my strange abilities right now. They were holding me on the edge of this boat with suction, amazingly, but I wasn't deliberately focussing on it. It just happened naturally!

The official-looking person appeared to walk into a more private part of the boat, so I crawled onto the main deck! I didn't have a clue what I was looking for, but I was simply following my instincts, whether they were reptilian or my usual ones!

My sense of smell seemed heightened. I could smell the aftershave of the man on the boat. I knew he was the only one on the boat!

How did I know that? I haven't a darn clue!

So, knowing that I only needed to keep out of view of this one man and attempt to hide from the overhead helicopter somehow, I decided to crawl into the sheltered parts of the boat.

There was an odd smell that I followed. I expected it to take me to the toilet, as it wasn't the most pleasant smell, but instead it took me to a section of the large sofa. I wasn't sure why, but with some defining sniffing, like a dog, I identified some kind of package.

My eyes were zooming in like some kind of robotic, enhanced vision! I identified some wires and sticky things on this package. I didn't fully understand it until there was a timer on the side.

"Shit... a bloody bomb!"

I needed to tell somebody! How was I going to do that looking like I did? I decided I needed to tell the man and do any explaining later!

"Hey! Hey!" I shouted around the boat, trying to find the touring man.

I smelt him out, remembering that skill! It made me chuckle inside however! He was then right in front of me, not paying any attention to me standing there.

"I've found the bomb, if that's what you're looking for?"

The man looked through me, but I could tell he heard my words. I couldn't waste any time, as I didn't know how long we had to escape.

"Hey! I need you to listen! I can see where the bomb is!"

The man looked left and right and reached forward to feel nothing. I wasn't that close. Was I invisible? This was crazy. I guess I just needed to guide him ultimately at this moment.

"There's a bomb under the sofa, in the main sitting area. Follow me!"

Again, the man obviously couldn't see me, but he finally decided to respond.

"Where are you?" His voice was extremely deep and powerful.

"I'm just in front of you. It doesn't matter, just go to the sofa and look underneath it!"

The man walked forward, not caring for my personal space now, so I skipped back swiftly to avoid him bumping into me.

I looked down at my hands and they were transparent.

What? I didn't get it. At least it explained the man's vision!

The man looked frightened, but tried to focus. He moved towards the sofa space and looked underneath it. His eyes grew large once he spotted the bomb! He radioed something into one of his team members somewhere. His voice was so appealing! I couldn't focus on that right now though! Perhaps since my so-called "changes", I had a higher sex drive, or appeal towards more dominant males. My mind was going off track again!

I heard the man say something about only having five minutes on the timer and needing to figure out the solution.

What? I didn't think we had five minutes!

It was sensible for me to reach past him and grab it. I knew I could take it far into the deeper seas, out of the way of everyone. The man stood up suddenly, shocked by the movement of the bomb.

It made sense for me to swim out to sea and allow it to explode away from everyone.

This seemed instinctive of me.

The man followed this bomb with his eyes, not knowing what was occurring.

I dived effortlessly into the sea and swam with great speed. I then noticed the timer that was mentioned. It was clocking down pretty fast. The seconds seemed to move faster than a regular clock. I could have sworn the seconds were going at milliseconds, not that I *actually* knew how to measure time!

I managed to swim deep into the ocean. I didn't even know where in the ocean I was! It didn't feel right however to murder a tonne of sea life, so I looked at the clock to see how long I had for alternate thinking. I had about a minute, going by super speed time! Thankfully I spotted an area that seemed dry under the deep sea! Not that I could quite fathom the meaning of *dry* rock or areas under water! It was just the emptiest space I could find in the sea!

I quickly found a space and allowed the bomb to begin to sink, slowly. At least the sinking was happening at a more preferred speed! Slower!

I swam as fast as I could in the opposite direction. My abilities were 'supersonic' it seemed when my usual adrenaline feeling kicked in.

I turned after a while to note a huge explosion of water lifting intensely. It was quite a significant amount of water shooting up. I could see all of this from below the water, from a distance.

I was suddenly questioning my mind again. How did I do this without question? How did I do this without any form of panic at all? It wasn't humanly possible, surely!

Either way, the issue was over and my next thought was that of trying to get back to Jason before he assumed I didn't want to be with him today! I remembered his quick ejaculation and how he may think I didn't want to be with him because of that! Ah, his precious ego could be playing games with his head right now.

I swam superfast back to the shore, remembering how quickly I could run, or crawl over the sand. It wasn't a certainty that I would still be transparent however!
I thought I would test my visibility with a crazy idea before taking to the shore.
Someone was surfing near me now, so I tapped the bottom of his board a few times, a bit like knocking on a door to get their attention. I floated underneath the water, looking up for their reaction.
The surfer looked over the edge of their board with panic. The male had really long hair which seemed to get in the way when tilting his head over each side. It was clear to me that he couldn't see me no matter how hard he looked.
I wondered then how long I was able to do this invisible trick! It would be a serious advantage - disguising myself from such horrifying features!
Thank you surfer!
I was now able to swim on shore and crawl over the sand swiftly to a safe point. There were some changing rooms up ahead, where I crept into a cubicle and waited patiently, calming any features if I could with my mind.

It only seemed to take a couple of minutes for my hands to change back into normal form! I listened for anyone else in the changing areas and noted complete silence enough for me to have a view of myself in the nearest mirror.

Thankfully, I looked perfectly normal! All except a re-alignment required to cover my boobs properly with my bikini top! It had twisted so much that I would have been completely exposed!

I walked back, feeling rather bizarre, but sexy at the same time having performed some amazing heroic act without anyone even knowing it! Thanks to "Jelly!"

I walked back to Jason, who was looking quite relaxed on his back, enjoying the sun. He was pleasantly surprised to see me.

"Ah, I wondered where you got to! Were they a little walk away?" He was genuinely concerned.

"Well, let's say I needed to head out a little further than expected but I was able to release the water!"

"That's good! I guessed you may have given up with finding the loos and just gone in the sea."

I chuckled at that idea, but couldn't help wonder if my toilet abilities might be different when I've converted into this strange being I become! Thankfully Jason didn't study me too hard because I still had some sea water drip drying from my body.

When we relaxed on the beach, I was now trying to formulate all of the crazy actions in my mind into some reasoning!

I noticed the helicopter flying further out, seeking the area of explosion. It went out quite a distance, making me realise the distance I had swum!

Then I chuckled to myself with the realisation of the crew trying to figure out the puzzle of the bomb.

I was trying to stop thinking and just relax now, but all of a sudden I realised the crazy surfer "gang" must've been the ones who were trying to get revenge with the people on the boat! Why would they take things to such extreme? I'm so glad I was here today. It was literally a life saver.

My mind calmed and I began to relax fully. Jason and I spoke casually between drifting off into lazy snoozes.

I was in one of those snoozes, when I woke to a dark shadow hovering above my face! It took a while for my eyes to focus on the face with the bright sun beating down around the features.

"Hello young lady. I didn't think you'd ever return."

Annie's voice was the first recognised feature.

I sat up and twisted to face her swiftly with shock!

"Annie! How did you find me amongst this huge crowd?"

She grinned at my words.

"Well, you look exactly the same as last time with your defining bikini and body shape. You're also lying on the same bright orange towel you came with last time we met."

"Oh yes, I guess it is quite a conspicuous towel, but I thought it was modern enough to blend into the other bright coloured towels on the beach."

I sensed Jason could feel the awkwardness in the tone. He decided to sit up too, maybe helping me feel supported.

"So, I was going to let you know about my next visit but this one is specifically for my boyfriend and I to chill."

"Don't worry, I get it. I thought I'd say hello anyway."

My words were basically telling her to sod off and leave us alone. I knew she was reading between the lines. She wasn't stupid, but she did seem to have obsessive behaviours of some sort. I didn't feel comfortable with her. She held some kind of sly smile. I wasn't sure why she was still stood over us, but I could see her mind ticking over.

"If you're interested later, we're having another party with food and drink if you both fancy joining us. I'm sure the guys would love to see you hooked up with this hunk. He'd put them to shame."

Jason smiled with appreciation but uncertainty. His thoughts were most certainly clear.

"Well..." I was about to explain that we were at the beach for some personal time, when Jason jumped in.

"We'll certainly consider it... the way to a man's heart and-all-that."

I shot a shocked look at Jason with the hope that it was him being polite and not submissive.

"Okay then. If it's a possibility then I look forward to catching up with you."

With that, she walked away with a very provocative strut. She knew she had an attractive body. I spotted Jason having a sneaky peek.

As soon as she was out of sight, I was hoping for a comforting conversation.

"You don't actually want to join that dodgy crowd I was telling you about did you?"

"Well I was thinking about the free food and the cool company, but not being too long to outstay our welcome. Unless you think they're particularly dangerous to be with. Following that we could head back to the hotel room to get that second attempt in." He started rubbing my arm up and down with seductive strokes.

"Jase, those guys are total dicks," I felt myself talking like a teenager. "They steal from that boat over there. In fact the boat crew and the surfers have some kind of vindictive vendetta against one another. It could end with serious consequences. We don't want to be part of that. Trust me."

"Ah, what? It sounds like the movies - a spot of exciting danger. I'm sure they won't clash at some party when they're miles apart."

I wish I could have told him some serious truths, but he seemed keen to be part of the cool surfer team, just as I initially did.

I was going to argue against it, but after a short few moments of him rubbing my arm and neck, I realised I could play detective amongst the crowd. Perhaps if I spent some spy-time with them, I could figure out their overall intentions with the boat people. With my adjusted viewpoint, Jason twisted with a decision to support my original dislike.

"Look, if you don't want to, we could just head back to the hotel. It's no problem. I'm genuinely fine either way, so long as I'm with you."

"Actually, it's okay. Let's do it. A bit of danger... you've talked me into it."

"You are a confusing lady Jen." Jason chuckled.

We managed to get some complete relaxation on the beach. We would occasionally acknowledge one another with a loving kiss and share a good swim with one another.

The evening came fairly quickly, forcing a cooler temperature. I wanted to suggest a new segment of events.

"Jase, how about we head back to our room to clean up, ready for an evening stuffing of food?"

I could see the surprise on his face suggesting he had hoped for more beach time.

"We can come back if you want to join the surfer crowd."

He grinned in agreement. I knew this social gathering was looking guaranteed. It made me feel nervous though, especially knowing that the surfer who pushed me off my board would be there. I hoped Jason knew how to take care of himself.

Why was I even risking this? Why did Annie have to come along yet again? Is she an innocent party? Or is she just a manipulator?

I suppose with these questions popping up in my mind, I wanted to play her at her own game. If I was to act like a "sucker" and join in with these events for a moment longer, then I could behave like an undercover police officer, gaining knowledge from the inside. The only risk was the police already being aware of the group's activities and getting involved enough to be "pinned" as another guilty party. I hoped one more innocent gathering would be safe enough.

Jason and I were packing up during my analysing thoughts.

We grew ready with our bag and surf board, ready to head back to the hotel room.

When we freshened up and prepared ourselves, it was nice to see Jason looking smart, but cool. I brought a summer dress along to attempt to impress him. We both enjoyed our views of one another. Jason moved in for a kiss and wanted to share another moment, but then moved back with the idea that he wanted to remain fresh for our food.

I checked that he definitely enjoyed the idea of the surfer's get-together. He seemed to love the idea of it, but wanted to ensure I was comfortable. I didn't really fancy it, but still felt the strange pull to gather information to stop their violent ways.

We toddled along, enjoying a lovely walk back in the direction of the beach.

We were approaching the group when Annie spotted us and lured us in with a great welcoming.

"Jenny! I'm so glad you came. We wanted to apologise for our first meeting. We shouldn't have involved you in such crap. Come and enjoy yourself with our food and drink. I have someone who wants to speak to you too." She pulled one of the men over by his loose sleeve.

I recognised the face of this man instantly and he made me feel sick for a moment.

"Look, I think you're cool and I'm sorry that I was such a dick."
He was obviously apologising for pulling me into the water during
our night surf.

"Well, you could've killed me, you're friggin' idiot." I couldn't
believe my instant response. I pushed him with both hands,
expressing my emotions. Everyone turned to see what the
commotion was and Jason looked horrified.

"Jenny! What are you doing?" Jason obviously didn't want his
perfect perception of a surfer party ruined.

The surfer looked shocked at my push and his crowd of friends
moved in, looking as if they were about to defend him.

Even *I* was shocked at my own actions, so I was swiftly thinking of
ways to turn the situation around. Thankfully though, I didn't
need to.

"Hey, I deserve that. I was an arsehole." He looked over at his
friends, "I deserve it guys, let's get these people a good drink!"
Jason looked at me with one raised eyebrow.

"What the hell?" He didn't look impressed.

"Shit. I'm sorry Jase. I think it was pent-up anger."

"Who are you?" He asked with such confusion.

Jason was soon moved by the spoiling actions of everyone
however, turning his gaze from me, to receive shoulder hugs and
drinks from these strangers.

Everyone mucked in, trying to offer food and drink to me, treating
both of us like a prince and princess. It was odd. Annie looked
over at me.

"If the big guy gives you respect, then you'll be treated well, so just
relax."

Jason looked at me with a big frown and whispered quietly into my ear.

"Is this some kind of weird gang?"

It did feel strange, but we took the abundant offerings of food and drink willingly. The group did come across as strangely childish, but since we were now here, it was tricky to simply walk away.

I whispered back in Jason's ear.

"Just enjoy the food for now. Enjoy being spoilt for a moment."

I could tell Jason agreed, but I hoped this wasn't freaky enough to push him away. This wasn't my normal behaviour, so I even questioned my own thinking.

Was I picking up their behaviours? Argh, just enjoy the food for a while, grab some obvious information and then sneak off.

Jason got into the sociable feel of this meal and spoke to a few of the men comfortably. They laughed and giggled, sharing talks of cars and the beach life. It all blended well.

Annie was behaving like my best friend. If I relaxed, I found this was all fun. I wanted these people to be as lovely as they generally seemed to be. It was my hope that they weren't the criminals I was judging them to be. All evidence led that way however, so I couldn't allow myself to get drawn in too much.

I wanted to emphasise to Annie that Jason and I were here to work on our romantic side, so not to expect us to stay too late. She didn't seem to behave in her usually addictive ways and gave a relaxed response.

I still needed to work on my collection of evidence. People were nattering so randomly that the subject I wanted to hear about wasn't popping up. I knew it wouldn't be an open discussion, but I was tuning into other people's conversations where I could.

It was growing late and Jason had his hooks into someone, having a very detailed discussion on motorbikes. I moved about, trying to find more discreet chatter. Two men were slightly distant from the main crowd, so I scuffled over, trying to catch word of anything unusual. As I moved, I looked casual with my food and drink.

These two were having a heated discussion near the shed area. It was difficult with my subtle moves to gain distance, but I managed in excitement to get relatively close. The man with the defined Mohican hair-cut spoke aggressively to a very fragile and skinny-looking surfer. I leant casually against a lamp post, within good earshot of the words. I wondered if I could fine tune the super-hearing ability at the same time. A sudden rush of noises came to mind.

Aha! It must be all about the focus and intention.

I was recognising the ignition of my abilities. I'd better not intend the gill on my arm or the webbed hands and feet, otherwise this dress would be holding some strange looking lady!

I focussed my hearing in. By luck, I caught word of some of their actions.

"...Why not?" The Mohican surfer was trying to encourage something.

"You twat, it won't work. We can't risk it again. They'll be onto it like hot shit!"
I caught the first set of words from the frail looking surfer. His mouth sounded tougher than his body.

"We have one left, let's get in there!"

"I don't give a shit how many we have left."
The frail surfer certainly had a big gob!

"How the hell can we sell the good stuff if we know they're still out on the hunt?"
I was trying to make sense of their conversation.

"Look man, we can still sell, it's too risky to try again."

I wondered what they were trying to sell and then the vision of the jewellery came to mind. Perhaps that was it. I listened on, but had interruption from another surfer joining in on the conversation.

"Hey, what are you two scheming over? Get some drinks in ya!"
This surfer was much perkier. I listened in for a moment longer. The Mohican man seemed a bit vexed.
"Don't you know when to knock?"
I chuckled at his words with having his conversation interrupted.
"What the hell? No need to jump down my throat."
"Ah, I'm sick of pussies around here. Get the hell out of my face."

I took a peek to note that he pushed the fellow surfer away and then walked off towards the shed.

I decided to tune out and walk casually in the opposite direction, falling into pleasant talks with joyful personalities.

I was pretty certain the surfers were involved in the attempted murder, or at least the attempted destruction of the boat. They were perhaps avoiding accusation of the jewellery thieving by taking drastic action. What deep situation have they gotten themselves into? Such troubled lives in exchange for greed.

I found Jason, looking at a bowl of crisps, seemingly between conversations. Perfect!

"Jase, can we go now? I was hoping for our more chilled-out version of this break."

He had a concerned look over my request.

"Ah my lovely, I'm so sorry, I thought we were enjoying this. Let's do a gradual fadeout then huh?"

I was so relieved to hear his suggestion, but hoped his fadeout version matched the ideal speed of mine!

Annie wasn't surprised by our casual goodbye. I felt good about the entire sequence of events, as in my eyes I had my revenge on the 'big guy' and discovered enough word to assume their guilt. Now, the words could be about something entirely different, but if they were then it would be *hugely* coincidental.

Jason and I were well fed, with a sensible amount of alcohol enough to continue on with a bit of fun of our own.

The hotel room still looked amazing, even if we had previously ruffled things up a bit. Jason began his passionate kissing and we stripped off, falling onto the bed. This felt wonderful. He seemed extra tenderly loving in his actions. We grew relaxed, which I hoped would help him achieve what he wanted. He looked a little bit too relaxed now and I noticed his eyelids growing heavy. *Noooo!*
Yup! He's asleep!

I couldn't believe it. Maybe the sex thing wasn't meant to be between us two!
He still had the morning if he wanted to try yet again.
I didn't bother to cover him up as he was on top of a cosy duvet that I needed half of!
Thankfully it didn't take me too long to drift off as well.

I woke the next day, long before Jason, feeling wonderfully refreshed and vibrant. The room was so comfortable and quiet. Everything felt tranquil.
I crept out of bed and managed one of my secret showers without being seen. Thoughts of disappointment filled me however, as a shared shower in normal circumstances may be good for us!

I was able to dress fully and look reasonable for the day. Jason was still completely out of it! I didn't think he drank that much. I'm not sure if this was something I needed to get used to, but either way, I couldn't lie there just loafing around.

Darn it I'm hungry.

I thought about breakfast, but didn't want to be selfishly scoffing away before he woke.

Time was ticking away and I didn't know what to do to entertain myself. The television screen looked at me, so I thought I'd see if I could watch something on mute or extremely low volume. I could test my super-hearing intentions out!

It was nearing eleven o'clock and I couldn't believe Jason was still sleeping! I decided I was going to head to the dining area to gain some breakfast. It was getting silly now. I didn't want to wake him up though, as then I'd have to wait yet again for him to get up and ready.

I crept out of the room and walked along the lovely corridors, bypassing a gym and swimming pool on the left. It looked very appealing.
Getting to the dining room, I asked for a large fry-up. The barman shocked me by saying breakfast was no longer served! I should have known, but it just didn't cross my mind. He offered a burger that had many of the contents of a typical fry-up, which I accepted gratefully.

As I ate, I spotted the familiar figure of Jason walking in.
"Oh, you *are* alive then!" I couldn't help myself.
It was like sharing a room with a teenager.

"Ah, I am so, so sorry! I forgot about the effects of beer. It knocks me out!"

"Alcohol does tend to do that."

"Ah jeez, I have ruined this weekend for you haven't I? I haven't met your expectations."

I began to feel guilty at this point.

"Oh, I'm sorry. I love the room and I enjoyed our time together. It has been a fun adventure. I'm only cranky because I'm such a fuss pot about routine. It's so boring really! I also get moody if I don't eat when I'm hungry."

"Hunger does tend to do that." He grinned with his cheeky grin.

He didn't seem bothered about ordering food, but helped himself to a glass of orange juice from the bar.

"Hey, we can do this again another weekend if you fancy giving it another go? Time with you, by the beach... it's heaven to me."

He encouraged me to smile broadly.

"Do you always waste the mornings with sleep though?"

"Ah no! In the week I'm up super early. In fact I was up really early yesterday and then drank way too much last night. I wouldn't have deliberately decided to lie-in on such a wonderful occasion. I just didn't think about my body's likeliness of needing super recovery. I was so disappointed when I woke up to find you weren't there. I couldn't believe the time! Shall we just stay here and chat, then order lunch?"

"I think it'll be more of a brunch, don't you? How long do we have the room for?"

"I held it until two P.M."

"Oh, that's good. I always remember it to be ten A.M."

"Sadly, the extra time wasn't free."

I felt so ungrateful at this moment.

"Jeez, you really have gone a distance to spoil me. I really appreciate that."

"My intention was truly to give you the best time ever."

He knew how to win me over.

"Thank you. I truly did have a great time with you."

"Hey, it isn't over yet young lady!"

"Ooh!"

I wasn't sure what he had in mind, but he was right, there was the rest of the day yet!

We decided to head back to the beach after a spot of brunch. It was quite crowded, but expected with it being such a beautiful day.

As we found ourselves lying on the beach, having a lovely soaking of the sun, the familiar shape of Annie came waltzing over to us yet again! I couldn't believe it!

"Hey guys! It was great to see you both last night! We try to have every Saturday together if you ever fancy joining in, in the future. Everyone likes you guys. You fit in well."

Why was she saying this?

I couldn't cause any trouble for fear of ruining our beach time, so I simply said, "ah thanks."

Annie didn't seem to accept that as final however.

"No, seriously, we feel you're part of our group. Please come any Saturday to join us for the same."

Jason tried this time. "Thank you very much Annie."

"Okay then. I hope to see you soon, whenever you're about."

She strolled off lightly on her feet, as if she was born to move easily across sand.

I turned to face Jason.

"Can you feel the same suspicion that I feel?"

"Huh? What do you mean?"

"Well, Annie has been super keen for me to be her best buddy. She's so over familiar."

"Oh, you know you are too much of an analyser. Just chill and enjoy being the focus of attention sometimes."

Maybe he was right. His tone was on the verge of being "fed up". I hoped I wasn't annoying him too much. He noticed my expression and decided to change the atmosphere.

"Come on let's try some of the surfing you're getting great at."

"Ah, I think I'll go in a bit later." My legs weren't quite ready for activity.

"Oh come on... Let's go and have some fun in the sea. The day is flying by. I have the need to have a little fun."

He was drilling the word "fun" into his sentences, which always pricked my ears up. He was right, I needed to lighten up.

"Alright then, but you have a go on the board first. You've got some catching up to do."

He reached over to grab me and imposed a dramatic tickling session. We laughed and fought to stand up.

Getting ourselves ready for the water, I remembered to put my arm support on. Jason didn't comment, but I could tell his glance always asked questions. I hoped my arm was the only thing I would need to hide!

The sea was cool and crisp, but just right for the warm temperatures.

Jason and I took long turns on the board, giving our legs chance to rest between.

After some hours had passed, my legs were begging me for a rest, so I decided to lie on the board when it was my turn. I wasn't prepared for the loud shout in my ear.

"What the hell is that?" Jason was shocked by something!

He was staring at the top of my back, so I turned to spot a blade-type shape forming from my spine, like a sharp fin! I could only see it from the side given my peripheral vision.

No! No!

Swift thoughts to explain what he could see flashed through my mind, but I couldn't think of anything.

"What is that? What is that?" He was shouting in panic.

Shit, now he knows I'm a freak! What do I do? What do I do?

I felt my adrenaline kick in and I needed to run!

He stared at my back, wanting to reach over, but I flipped backwards into the sea and swam faster than ever into the depths! I could feel my bikini bottoms slipping down to my ankles, but at this point it didn't seem to matter! The panic was intense. My weirdness had slipped out! My biggest nightmare had occurred! What the heck was I going to do?

I swam and swam, feeling my super strength kick in stronger than ever before. There was no time for my analytical mind right now. I just needed to get away!

After several minutes I felt the need to stop. I lifted my head to find myself in the deepest parts of the sea. It didn't bother me, but I was just attempting to gain my bearings. I was in so deep that there was no land to be seen! Boy, I was now in with the dolphins and the sharks. I didn't know what level of prey or predator I was in the sea world!

Shit! Now what?

My whole world suddenly felt upside down and irreparable. I thought that if I kept swimming in the same direction that perhaps I would eventually get to another country, where I could start again, maybe living a primal life with fish as my staple diet! How weird would that be? No Yoga; no friends or family to see. What if my best friends would now be sea life, making conversation with Eels or starfish? What?

Nooo! I'm a weirdo and I need answers! What have I become?

Who the hell am I?

Jelly! I am Jelly!

I reached the shore of some empty, quiet rough land. It was perfectly private, but I didn't have a clue where I was.

I had a desire to pick from the rocks and eat from the small ponds, so I did it, filling myself with sea life!

My body felt full and tired as it slowly converted back to the human state I was used to. I tried to calm myself with thoughts of safety and peace.

I must have dozed off. My eyes and brain slowly formed the colours of the sky and clouds, but the brightness was fading. I pushed myself up to a seated position on a patch of rough grass, only to note a young man with long scruffy hair staring at me intensely!

"Oh, err it's not how it looks. I just got lost at sea."

Now that was already a weird thing for me to say.

He looked down into my leg area. That's when I remembered I had lost my bikini bottoms.

"Oh my gawd! I lost them on the way. The current took them when I was swimming for survival. Will you help me with a towel or something?"

He stared on without words for a moment, eventually deciding to walk away.

It was strange that he didn't offer one single word.

I was relieved that he had departed however.

While I had privacy, I hunted around rough vegetation to see if there was anything I could use to cover myself up. I couldn't find anything other than the obvious leaf, but I would need to hold it in position.

Where the hell was I?

The ground was relatively rough underfoot, but then I wasn't used to walking around barefoot very often.

I caught sight of another figure coming down a steep part of this piece of land that I had encountered. This figure held a staff and walked bow legged. I assumed the person to be of the male species, as he had quite a broad chest.
I tried to hide behind bushes, but this figure was still walking directly toward me. My nerves kicked in and I considered another running-dive back into the sea.
"Jenny!" The voice was very deep and robotic.
How the hell did he know my name?
I remained tucked behind some bushes, curious, but ready to run and swim.
"I know you need some answers and I can give them to you."
What? Answers?
"We have been waiting for you to ask in the most private of places."
Ask what?
At this time, I noticed a bright ring of light form around my space. It made me look at the sky for an explanation.

"We can explain everything. We just need a moment of your time."

I tried to escape, but bumped into some kind of invisible wall! Before attempting again, I felt around with my hands to notice that the ring around me was actually the base of some circular tube I now found myself standing in.

"I'm sorry about the containment. It is for your own safety. We need you to listen. I plan to tell you gently. We mean absolutely no harm."

I felt like a trapped mouse, collapsing into a heap of submissive despair, knowing my predator had captured me.

The figure was up close now and I was brave enough to catch sight of the details of them. He was tall but slightly bent over. He had very sharp, deadly looking spikes coming out of him from most parts. His eyes were large, with thin, orange pupils that moved horizontally across a set of deep brown eyes. His feet were heavily webbed and he looked as if he had a small wingspan from his shoulders. His head was quite spiked too, with simply holes for his nose. The mouth looked extremely lethal, with teeth that were obviously razor sharp. His staff looked glowing in certain areas across the entire length. The colour of his body appeared to change from dark shades of grey, to green and brown, almost blending too much into the scenery.

I don't think I was breathing at this point. The shock of yet more extremely unusual events were hitting hard.

This "person" pressed a button on his staff and the invisible cage that I appeared to be in, lit up with blues and purples. It was so beautiful that it mesmerised me. I suddenly felt a strong sense of calm.

"I'm sorry about the tube you are in. It is to keep you safe and calm for only a few moments, then you shall be set free once again."

The voice was still deep and robotic, but it didn't faze me this time. This colourful, tripping experience was wonderful. I was still completely aware, yet anything could have happened and I knew I would still remain calm. If there was an amazing drug to be found, then this would be it! I sat down with a *pleasant* version of lethargy.

"We need to feed you some answers."

"Feed me?"

I listened despite my judgement on their choice of words.

"You have been part of a circumstance that you were not meant to experience."

"Well I know that!" I realised I was being cheeky, so quickly sealed my lips tightly. I decided I needed to shut up and listen. His stare was intense and strong.

"We have put you in an extremely difficult position."

I wanted to say that my life was *only* ruined, but I decided to continue to seal my lips.

"We have been visiting your planet and now successfully understanding your language."

It's clear you're a friggin' alien, but I'm not sure you sound successful with our language.

I was still extremely calm.   My hope was that they weren't able to hear my thoughts.

"Our secret experimentations have been perfectly successful, all except our error with *you.*"

He still sounded very robotic.

As he spoke, another 'creature' crept down into the area... one that looked slightly smaller. If I was to be open about my initial impression of the second alien, then I would say that he or she looked quite gentle and delicate. They too held some kind of staff with different coloured lights all of the way through.

Are they going to get to the point of all of this?

The powerful, robotic voice introduced me to the smaller alien.

"This is Shmea 3289."

I listened on without judgment of their naming methods!

"Shmea 3289 came to you one night with intent to retrieve some blood cells in order to understand human evolution."

"Okay."

"You woke during the time of the procedure. You were not meant to feel or sense the presence of Shmea 3289."

"Well, I'm sorry, but maybe my sensing is part of my evolution!"

I didn't want to apologise for *their* intervention! How dare they mess with my body!

"On this planet we request consent for anything that may be intervening! I did not give you any form of permission!" I felt slight anger, but didn't have the strength to fight.

The smaller alien looked very sheepish.

The larger alien continued to explain.

"If we can understand you better, then our entire Universe can grow and evolve. Your 'kind' may be behind in technology, but you are evolving *generally* at a fast pace, changing continually with your expansion of awareness."

"Maybe so, but it doesn't give you the right to help yourself to my body, particularly when I am trying to rest." I recalled the dream of the doctor and waking to the smear of colour swiftly disappearing. I also recalled the second dream of the alien face! "It wasn't just a dream then! You were poking around my arm! You're the reason my life has turned upside down and inside out!" I realised my 'lip sealing' plan wasn't 'going to plan'!

The smaller alien looked over his or her shoulder, obviously contemplating departure.

"Shmea 3289 wishes to rectify the situation for you. You have some choices, based on your preference."

"What choices? My first choice is for you to fix me and then send me back home."

The large alien looked disappointed!

"We have these choices. You may come to dwell with us on our planet, where we all share the same abilities. There you will enhance our knowledge and *yours*. You will be treated with much abundance. Our planet is wonderful."

I couldn't believe what I was hearing!

"So what abilities do I have? I have discovered the gill and the webbed feet and hands... I think there's some kind of thing on my back sometimes, a blade or something!"

"You are able to swim, crawl, glide, climb, run, jump, – all with great speed, lightness, breathing and strength. You can detect and scan. All of your senses are enhanced."

"What do you mean by glide? Do you mean in the water?"

"We mean in the air."

"I can fly?"

"When it is urgent for you to save yourself from falling, then you can glide."

"What?"

"When necessary, you can glide through your air."

"Through the sky?"

"Yes."

"What?"

I couldn't believe it. We were all silent for a moment while I tried to digest some of the information I received.

I felt it was my turn to speak.

"What other options do I have?"

"You can stay, but your features pose great risk for your freedom."

"You mean there's a risk I may become an experiment?"

"This change may cause many difficult circumstances that would make your life unhappy. You being here on this part of land is already the beginning of such seclusion."

"You mean I'm likely to become an outcast?"

"We see that you have begun that process, yes."

"Is there a way that you can reverse what you did to me?"

"We have never been in such circumstance. Shmea 3289 needed to remove small amounts of your cells, but with shock of your waking instead added some of Shmea 3289's cells into your body."

"How can that happen with a needle?"

"A needle?" The alien didn't understand the idea.

"Shmea 3289 would normally open a section of the finger and allow cells to enter a sheath in the finger for containment until returned to the transportation, where this can arrive into further containment."

"What?" I didn't understand.

The smaller alien lifted a hand and showed me a finger. The end of their finger opened slightly. It opened to look a bit like a very, very small elephant's trunk. A sharp needle-styled item came through the middle briefly and then moved back. The very, very small opening then closed tightly shut after a short moment. I was mesmerised.

I sat there very aware of the leaf covering my pubic hair, thinking this wasn't too strange after all!

"So the ends of your fingers can open up to collect items and then seal again?"

"Precisely. We can collect many items of our choosing. This can be for discovery, experimentation or food collection."

I laughed quite hard.

"That is so funny!"

The aliens both looked on with innocence and misunderstanding.

"So, instead of sucking my blood out, Shmea, or whatever the name is, put something inside me?"

"Precisely. This has never happened during any of our expeditions."

I felt like asking so many questions, such as how many "expeditions" they had been involved in.

"So you say you haven't had this situation before, so I am stuck with my new mixture of blood? You mean I can't even go to a doctor for a blood test if I have an issue, without them discovering I have unusual blood?"

"This is why you are offered the opportunity to live in our community. We feel that you would appreciate our hospitality. There will no longer be any concerns for you."

"Well I can't decide without knowing what your planet is like! I might hate it. If I decide to stay here and live as normal as I possibly can, would it mean constant observations from your life forms?"

"We have already discovered the effects of mixing our blood with yours, even though this was in error, so we would have no need to interfere with your life again, unless you *offer* yourself for further experimentation. We do wish to continue to experiment with your species generally. If you did decide to come with us, then you can live freely. We would respect any decision you made. The law of choice cannot be broken with any species."

I was mostly confused, but tried to concentrate.

"So I am stuck with this either way? "

"You see this in a negative state, however, when you decide to convert to a positive state, you will find this is an advantage to you."

I pondered for a moment. It would be interesting to see how this species lived! I then thought about my friends, family and my new potential boyfriend (provided I could explain the thing he saw on my back!). The love pulled me back, yet the intrigue pulled me forward.

"Is there a way I could visit you, but stay here?"

The alien paused.

"There is a way. You could take part in some simple training which could enable you to control your abilities better on Earth, but the risk is your mind set. It is easy for you to isolate yourself as I mentioned... and as you have already done. There are many risks, but there is the option to attempt it."

I noticed the tone of voice from this alien never changed.

"Hang on just a second though... How do I know this isn't one big hoax?"

"Can you explain it otherwise?"

"I can't."

"Are your eyes deceiving you?"

"My eyes aren't, but it could be my mind."

"You are fine. We have administered gentle mind calm."

Gentle mind calm? I kind of figured something to that effect anyway.

There was another strange pause. A valid question needed to be asked.

"So what happens now?

"Have you fully decided on what you wish?"

I thought again about everyone I loved and knew that I needed to stay on Earth.

"I think I shall stay here but visit you when we mutually agree."

"You are welcome in our world at any time. You just need to call for us. You have a natural ability to send out a signal. It will become apparent when it happens."

A panic hit me, despite mentioning it slightly before.

"What do I do if I have a health issue?"

"We are the ones to come to. It will also aid us with this new experiment that we did not intend to have."

"So, you may not have the cure? I will be an experiment if I get ill?"

"Well, we have more advanced technology. It is what you will need."

They seemed pretty convincing.

"Okay, so how do I visit your planet? And how do I get back to the beach I swam from? How do I explain things to my boyfriend?"

"Do you wish to visit our planet now, in your state of calm?"

"I guess that could work."

I didn't even feel an ounce of apprehension.

Both aliens appeared to play with buttons on their staffs, which created new colours to filter through the tubing I sat in. It was extremely beautiful.

A transparent roof appeared to form over the top of the tube and a rush of unexpected wind lifted me slightly from the ground. The formation of a bottom part of the tube moved through. I realised they were basically sealing the tube at the top and bottom. This tube literally began to lift, carrying me directly vertical into the sky. It hovered slightly before the aliens made some strange movement with their staffs, creating a tornado effect around them. Before my eyes, they disappeared and I suddenly found that I was high up off the ground.

Without any sensations in my body or mind, I shot up in unexplainable speed, directly upwards. The tube must have held some kind of amazing pressure inside to keep me perfectly intact. I knew this wasn't made of any Earthly inventions. It wasn't glass or plastic. All I knew was that it was transparent and strong enough to withstand anything it seemed.

I was still extremely calm, but did wonder how this was going to work. It was being in the hands of these friendly aliens. Perhaps I should focus on the words "friendly".

Surprisingly this transportation device didn't take me though any outer space darkness. It stopped at a height that I could imagine was slightly above aeroplane flight paths. I didn't seem to fear the height and enjoyed looking at the scenery of white fluffy clouds and green blends of land below, and the blue sky around me.

As I hovered in one place, the tube opened somehow, like a doorway in front of my eye view. I still felt comfortable in every respect. I heard a deep, male voice directly in front of me.

"Now this may seem very strange to you, but we are currently invisible to your eyes. I'm going to reach out and touch your hand and guide you through a corridor. You're going to need to trust me."

As the voice completed the sentence, I felt a very gentle hand touch mine and clasp underneath to encourage my palm compliance. My other hand tried to retain a steady hold on the disguising leaf! My bottom would be in bold view right now!

I stood and felt a gentle tug with his hand.

I felt myself pull back.

"It's okay, there is a floor. It's just invisible. It will make sense to you in a moment."

I could feel my face screwing up with confusion, as I took the first step out of this tube. This was strange. I felt solid ground under my feet, but there was no sign of ground with my eyes.

"How?"

"It will all make sense in a moment." His voice was so comforting. Why couldn't he have been the one to greet me initially?

I looked back to notice the tube blending into "nothing".

Looking down was the same view I had when inside the tube! Thankfully I still felt really calm. I don't know if it was something that lasted for some time once administered somehow. I don't even understand *how* it was administered! I may even be drugged up with some hallucinate. This might not even be real!

The kind voice started again.

"Now then, everything will be dark for just a few seconds okay? So just keep holding onto my hand. Everything is just fine."

Just as he explained this, a complete darkness surrounded me.

"What?"

"It's fine. Honestly, just a few seconds longer."

I waited patiently to see what he was trying to explain. I noticed glimmers of silver all over now. I couldn't explain anything myself! Just as I noticed the glimmers of silver, some low lights were beginning to reveal a floor beneath my feet. It was of pure white. I looked down to stare, but then looked up to see a lot of figures moving around. There weren't too many to make me feel crowded, but there were certainly a few. I could see that these figures were much the same as the two aliens, yet there were different coloured figures. Some were grey, some a blueish colour, some a pale yellow and some a green mixed with grey. They were all different heights and widths, with some twice as high as any human I've seen.

I was still holding onto this kind hand, but now I could view the character right in front of me. He had an almost-human like face, but his body was most certainly the same as the initial two aliens. He spoke again with kindness.

"Now then, you need an explanation. Come to sit in the calm room. It's a place that induces constant calm."

I was aware of my naked bum about to sit on their posh furniture!

"Just how does this calm thing work?"

"Well, there are fine particles that your human eye can't identify. They enter through your eyes, ears and generally your skin. It is so powerful that it hits you almost instantaneously.

"Wow! So it is a drug."

"Well, not in the same way that you identify a drug. We use it given natural sources from our planet. Our planet has all healing items supplied in its' nature. Yours does too, however you are yet to discover that."

"So, can I soak up as much of that calm stuff as I want? I can't overdose?"

"We have never known anyone to over dose."

I was so stunned by their amazing technology and aid for
themselves so far.

This alien-friend walked me across the white floor, over to some
silk covered seats. He instructed me to sit, kindly, so I did, only to
find that as soon as I sat on this amazingly comfortable chair, that
it blended to my shape, comforting me gently. I continued to
retain the position of the leaf!

"Ooh! Is this chair safe for me too?"

"Everything is safe in here. Trust me."

I sat comfortably, wondering what surprises were yet in store for
me. Within a short while of sitting, I was offered an item of white
material to wrap around my body. It wasn't too different from a
towel, yet had strings to tie sections together. I stood
momentarily, encouraging the chair to return to its normal shape.
I figured something out with this material to comfortably cover
my lower body parts! I looked down to notice that the chair
seemed to hold some form of intelligence. It appeared to vibrate
slightly, waiting for my bum to re-apply itself. I carefully sat again
to allow a re-moulding of comfort.

"Let me explain what has just happened. I am the leader on this
transportation. My name is Frush67."

"Frush67? Am I in a space ship?"

"If that is what your language would describe it to be, then yes."

"So far you know about our friend, Shmea 3289. I shall repeat the
information you have been given...

The natural fear response of Shmea 3289 is to push anything
outward, so the error was made when taking blood from your arm.

In fear of you waking, Shmea 3289 pushed your blood back, along with some of Shmea 3289's tissue. This resulted in you receiving particles in your blood stream that is powerful enough to give you the abilities that *we* have, given our DNA. This isn't something we have ever done before. In fact our cells are so advanced that it would have a huge impact on your body. This is why you have been developing added abilities. There is much more to it than that, but this is the easiest way to explain. It was an error created in fear. In exchange we offer you two worlds in which to live. It was understandably your decision to live on Earth, but visit our world at your leisure."

I already mostly understood the basics of what had happened, even though it was too crazy to take in fully at this moment in time. He continued...
"When visiting us, you will need to join in complete secrecy, where we can collect you using the process we already have done. Our ability to go unseen is a great technology. The transportation vehicles, such as your individual transport and this large group transportation vehicle can go undetected in your world. It appears unseen to your eyes until we decide to bring things into view. This would be when we know we are back in our own range of home. We move faster than your world currently knows of, so we can move from your atmosphere, swiftly into our own atmosphere. The distance is more than you can comprehend, but the neep is very brief."
"The neep?"

"Oh, that is our measurement of past, present and future. It takes very little neep to travel a large distance."

"Do you mean that it takes very little time for you to travel a great distance?"

"If *Time* is the same as *Neep*, then yes. We may have miss-matched words, but we mostly understand your language. It is a bit like your divisions on land having different languages, accents, phrases and sayings."

"Okay, that is fine. I understand so far. So are we currently a long way away from Earth?"

"More than you can understand. Our technology is extremely advanced. We discovered your planet a short neep ... *time*... ago, but we still haven't calculated how you evolve in your way. We evolve in a different way. It is useful to experiment other planetary ways."

"Well, we have always suspected that life on other planets exists. We know that some people like to hide the truth from us."

"It certainly does exist, as you can see! If you visit frequently, then you will witness our many experiments in different areas."

I looked around this "transportation" and noted how cold and plain everything seemed. There didn't even seem to be any buttons or levers anywhere. Everything seemed white and bright, but it felt so cold.

"You can view our planet any time you decide. Do you think you are ready to see this?"

"Are we on your planet now?"

"This is what I am explaining. It takes very little *neep* to arrive to our home. That is why one moment you were in the Earth's atmosphere and the next you were here."

I chuckled in my mind at how funny this whole situation was. I looked into the eyes of this new friend to note the features properly now that I could focus a little clearer. He had the shape of a human head, with the odd bit of wiry hair. His eyes were the same shape and direction of pupils that the first two aliens had, yet the pupil was black and the surrounding eye colour was a blood red! There were no white parts of the eyes to any of these beings. It was a little bit freaky to soak into my mind. His forehead had many thick, green veins to it, but his skin was almost human-like, with a tinge of green. His neck was thick and strong, with the funny spike features protruding outward. I could compare these spikes as a similar aspect to a hedgehog. All of the aliens that I'd seen here so far had two arms and two legs, with a body in the middle, similar to human bodies. These beings were crossed between lizards, hedgehogs, alligators, humans and goodness knows what. They were a strange sight to my eyes, but the first thought of my judgement was not to hold anything similar to "racism", since this "person", Frush67, appeared to hold much kindness.

"Do you wish to come to view our planet?"

He reached his hand out to me.

"Gosh, how could I refuse?"

Just as I met my hand with his, the chair retracted to its normal shape and I realised that I was comfortable in this material that covered my private areas!

We walked across the pure white floor, which didn't appear to give a noise of footsteps. It felt solid, but sounded as silent as walking over a "memory foam mattress!"

Frush67 spoke again.

"If you hear strange noises, do not be alarmed. There are some unseen doors that open and close during our journey. They are for our security and can be seen at our time of choosing."

"Okay." I felt like a child walking with a parent.

"Please also be aware that our language is of noise signals and sounds that a human's ears will not pick up. Just because you may not hear or see something, it doesn't mean that it doesn't exist. Sadly humans are quite weak in their five senses. Your sixth sense is however extremely powerful, but unused."

"Interesting," Frush67 seemed very wise.

We walked while I was only able to see pure white surroundings and the occasional alien roaming around.

Frush67 wanted me to be aware of something.

"Please look down at this moment and walk onto that new platform. This platform will move us slightly faster, so do not be alarmed. It is a moving walkway."

I looked down to see a matching white piece of floor that wasn't raised or lowered, just the given shape that we would need to stand on, like an outline!

"Oh, we have something similar in airports. Yours looks much more advanced, but we call them Travellators.

He didn't respond to my comparison.

"Please hold onto my hand just for safety."

I needed to hold his hand, but having sight of his hand this time felt a bit freaky. His palm seemed to have miniature lights of various colours shining outwardly. I couldn't hold the question inward.

"How come you have little lights in your hand?"

"Ah, very observant of you... We are able to give out particular energy through our hands, but it is visual and powerful. At this particular time I am releasing some calming energy for you, so that when you experience anything new, you feel good. All physical beings are energy and are able to give particular energies outward. Our levels are very advanced by comparison however, but only because we have focussed on enhancing this ability over a long period of time. We can administer all good things such as happiness, love and calm. Can you feel the calm?"

"Weird. I truly can." I felt a huge sense of calm fill me once again. We stepped onto this "travellator" and suddenly flung forward very swiftly. I looked down slightly to notice how well-gripped Frush67's webbed feet were to the ground. I thought it was funny to see my feet wobbling around, trying to keep still.

We were moving swiftly! I wished I had a means of measuring the speed. If I had my head sticking out of a car window right now during movement, then my hair would be blowing slightly!

The travellator slowed to a point, where something opened up before my eyes, to expose a fresh bit of land. We stepped off this travelling machine, onto a soft ground.

All of a sudden, everything appeared to open up to a huge space of freedom! The land was soft, but firm enough to walk along. There was a bright sky of silky blue and purples. It took a time to focus on everything, as there was too much to take in all at once. I looked down to see rivers of colours that I couldn't quite comprehend. The colours also seemed to give off a wonderful feeling as I walked over them. It felt as if I was walking along cool, marble effects under foot, but visually, I could see blends of such amazing vibrant colours. These blends were close to our golds, reds and purples, with streams of blues.

Looking ahead there were strange, transparent-type lifts that the aliens were walking into and shooting off somewhere rather swiftly. I asked Frush67 what everyone was doing. He told me that they could transport themselves off to different parts of the planet very swiftly. They could meet one another on the other side of the planet within seconds.

"Wow! This is all a bit like our television programme of Star Trek!"

"Well, I can imagine it is all a bit mind bending for you at the moment. There is much we have very different here compared to your planet. In fact some planets are much more advanced than even we are."

I realised Frush67 and I were still holding hands. It felt so comforting, so I wondered if he was still pumping something through me to help my level of calm. He noticed my thoughts. "Feel free to release your hand if you so choose, but you will benefit from my calm signals during this surprising time."
I agreed and continued to hold his hand.

We walked about, allowing me to soak some of the views in. There were strange lives on this planet. The aliens I grew familiar with were in the majority, but there were other smaller creatures moving around that I would attempt to focus on. They appeared similar to the animals I was familiar with on Earth, but they had such mixtures of features. One of them I couldn't help staring at had rabbit ears, with a nose as long as an ant eater and eyes as large as lightbulbs! It had three legs in a tripod form that scuffled around a bit like a spider! Strangely, I didn't feel frightened by all of the different creatures. They made me laugh quietly inside in fact!

I had a tour for quite some time and felt my legs begin to ache slightly. Frush67 noticed my slowed walking and made a strange noise outward, which induced a speedy vehicle to spring up in front of us within an instant! I recognised it as a vehicle, but it looked like a wide scooter with lower handles. The entire thing seemed to be made of silver and gold that glimmered. At the back of this scooter-like transporter, it had two half-moon shapes assumingly for our bums to sit back into. I looked closer to note that there were no wheels! So perhaps the 'scooter' comparison wasn't strong enough. It was more like a board with some handles at the end.

Frush67 guided me to sit on this machine, confirming for me to tuck my bum back into one of these half-mooned shaped parts. The half-moon part was slightly raised, comforting my lower back. A part of this vehicle dropped to allow our feet to sink in slightly. The gold and silver colours merged to melt almost, moulding our foot shapes into place. This all happened really swiftly, but I observed it closely. I knew I most certainly wouldn't understand this world over night! Then it "dawned" on me. Does this place have night and day... or seasons? It just seemed too bright and vibrant with all of the colours and the life force.

This scooter-type or board-type thingy moved swiftly with some hovering method. It was so smooth. If I could eat that smoothness it would be something similar to the chocolate brand of Galaxy! Galaxy silk! It was so appropriate.

We moved swiftly back into the surrounds of the great, bright whiteness of the transportation vehicle that we originally emerged from.

Frush67 explained that I needed gradual introduction as a human, so to come back in to rest for a while. We found a different resting area, with bright white mattresses to relax on.

I wanted to ask so many questions but didn't know where to begin.

"Don't stress yourself with trying to understand everything all at once." He spoke calmly, guiding me to relax on one of these mattresses.

I sunk into this mattress, feeling so amazingly comfortable... so much so that it was indescribable.

Frush67 wanted to explain something further.

"We wish to show you how to control your abilities so that you can live comfortably on Earth. When would like to begin this training?"

I grew excited. This would be my new lease of life!

"How long will this training take?"

"Oh, in Earthly Neeps, it will only take seconds."

"What?" I didn't know how to comprehend that. "How can I learn something within seconds?"

"In your understanding we can download information into your mind. You may not be able to explain it verbally, but you will be able to just *know*."

"Do you do something horrible to me?"

"Horrible?"

"Is it a nasty procedure?"

"Oh no, it is a simple transmission using the lights in my hands as you describe them to be."

"Hey? That is crazy!"

"It isn't something new, but humans are mostly unaware of this."

"So you can just put your hand lights on me?" I laughed again in my mind.

"We can, but first, we need you to be in a deep state of relaxation. It is purely safe, but we need to have trust with one another."

"Wow! Okay, well we've come this far!"

"There is what you would call a *booth* for you to sit within for this process to succeed."

"I'm willing to sit in a booth!" I wasn't sure if the mattress was giving off even more calm, but I didn't care about any booth or transmission of knowledge. All I knew was that it would be useful to control my abilities on Earth, so that I could live a normal life, but come here to set my abilities free!"

Once again I found myself holding onto Frush67's hand, walking over to a different scene of transparent booths, all sat in a row, horizontally. They simply looked like booths made of clear glass, or plastic.

"Err, have you done this before? I thought I was the only converted human, so-to-speak."

"These spaces are where we choose to rest and recuperate. We don't sleep as such, we just recharge, a bit like you would see a battery do."

"Oh! So I need to be in a sleepy state and then you put your lights on my head?"

I noticed Frush67 didn't show any signs of humour. My words must have been quite strange to him, but he didn't comment on the difference. I was beginning to crave the Earthly ways all of a sudden. It's wonderful how humanity can come together with humour and love. Although this was a wonderful experience, there seemed to be something missing here. Either way, I was willing to accept that I needed help at this time. I was cross for a moment, remembering that none of this was even my fault! Shmea-what's-a-face made a huge error! Mind you, what an unusual and fun experience to be had if I tilted things the other way up! I wanted fun and I most certainly had it in the strangest of ways! Perhaps I actually attracted this situation to me somehow. All of these things crossed my mind with the slow approach to one of the booths.

"There is a chair that you cannot see with your Human eyes, so feel for this with your hands before you sit. It is directly ahead within the booth."

I felt for the transparent chair and sure enough a solid shape was felt under my hands. It was odder than standing on those glass floors, looking down from a great height!

"Now find relaxation and sit comfortably."

I personally would have said that the other way around, but it didn't matter!

A feeling of drunken heaviness hit my mind, forcing me into a deep sleep. I wasn't aware of much at all, but I do remember vivid images and colours flying across the front of my eyes.

It seemed only a few seconds, just as Frush67 had said, before I woke to a fully conscious state, feeling extremely vibrant!

"Wow! Is this complete?"

"It is. How does this now feel?"

"Well, I can do this!"

I stood to push some small wing spans from somewhere at the back of my shoulder blades and instantly took to higher levels, like a low-flying bird!

"Way hay!" I expressed excitement, gliding freely through this plane white spaceship.

I knew the dimensions and all locations of this spaceship too! My knowledge was excessive! I didn't even understand how I knew everything. The material around my body flapped through the fast movement. I didn't care about flaunting anything at this time. Frush67 watched on without surprise.

"Okay, so you know of your abilities and about our transportation methods. Next time we can provide information on our species and planet."

As I glided I spoke.

"I want to know everything! This is amazing!"

"Please come down and speak with me about your return to Earth."

This guy seemed pretty boring, but then this would be a normal visual occurrence for him, other than me being mostly human!

I complied with his request and settled on the ground. I couldn't help play with my feet though while he tried to have a serious conversation with me. I could change my feet to their human state, straight into the webbed state within a second. It was absolutely fascinating to me.

"So you know that you have a signalling ability to call upon us, a bit like your bat creatures with their radar-type sensing. It works similarly, but you know how to use this form of communication naturally now."

I did! The ability was fresh in my mind. I felt some kind of vibe from me, like some invisible frequencies pushing outward. It was my only way of understanding it if I could describe it from my human brain. It was like invisible rings of Saturn around me, as if I was a planet in the middle. I was accepting of all of this pretty swiftly, but I would say that normally, a human wouldn't be able to cope with so much change! With that thought, Frush67 explained further.

"I will be administering something that will send you back to Earth with an ongoing calmness, but sharpness that will keep you in good balance."

I was suddenly aware of time, or "neep", as he called it.

"How long have I actually been here by the way?"

"In human time, only a few minutes."

"Oh my! I have left my boyfriend worrying about whether I am alive or dead!"

"He will be fine. We plan to send you back to your starting point."

"How do I explain what he saw?"

"We noticed that he witnessed your back blade, which enables you to swim with such speed. You can use the reason for someone's water toy part sticking to you accidentally."

Do these aliens miss a trick?

I realised his suggestion of explanation may just work.

"He will most certainly believe you, as most humans need a logical reason for everything."

I craved the love of Jason and the life I created on Earth. This was fun, but I now wanted a spot of normality. I'm not sure if normality will ever be part of me now, but anything near it would be welcomed.

"I feel it is time for you to return to your home. You will feel refreshed and well once you arrive. You are welcome to feed your knowledge here whenever you desire. You are now our Earthly friend. All choices are purely yours."

The alien appeared to smile, with a slight tightness in the lower part of his eyes. I wasn't completely certain though!
I had another silent chuckle inside.
It was strange at this point, as I could sense that I was about to head back down in the tubular transportation device!

Frush67 spoke of our next actions.
"This is the final time I need to hold your hand in order to administer complete calm for this to be ongoing for you."
He reached out, kindly meeting my hand. I noticed the brightness of various colours pushing out, even when our hands were clasped.
"Wow!" I knew how this worked now, but it was still a beautiful sight.

We reached a point where I could finely see the outline of the tubing transport. The opening was relatively clear, so I willingly stepped in.
"It has been a pleasure to meet you." I offered.
"And we shall most definitely meet many times again." He comforted me.

"Our accident with Shmea 3289 has created an amazing combination of human and Weezon. You are an example of something even greater than we imagined. We can now learn from this experience to become even more advanced."

I picked up on the word "Weezon" more than anything else he had said. I instantly knew that this was their label for *their* life form.
He continued...
"Would you be willing to provide a blood sample during one of your visiting occasions? It is also painless, but it would help us tremendously. Following that, we shall ask no more."

I grinned, knowing that these "Weezons" were very kind.
"Well, I suppose, if it helps somehow."
"Your offerings of assistance to us will help not only our planets, but all of the Universes."

Now that part I couldn't fully comprehend, but it sounded great! I was about to say something else, when I felt a mild pressure of the door closing. Lights emerged all around me again, bringing great comfort.
Frush67 walked slowly away and the spaceship turned to darkness, with the silvery shimmers all around.
Before I had time to even study this, the blue sky of the Earth surrounded me.
"Wow! Star Trek!"

I dropped very comfortably through clouds now, getting lower and lower until I reached a private part of a huge beach.

People were mingling on the sand in the distance. I wondered if I was invisible at this point. There was no way of telling. I apparently didn't have the eyes to see or not see! Although, I did see the door of this vessel open up widely for me to step onto the sand.

I actually felt quite nervous about the first step onto Earth's sand! I felt as if I had been up in the world of weirdness for longer than I was! I felt as if I had been on that other planet for an entire day! This needed to be done otherwise I would forever live in the transparent tube, hoping to be between worlds somehow. I couldn't live in limbo. I screamed inside and placed one foot out onto the sand. All Earthly feelings filled me, healing me of any concerns. The alien did say that I would feel calm, but I think I needed that first step after such unusual events. I didn't want to imagine how bad I would have felt *without* any calming remedies.

The sand felt wonderful between my toes, just like a natural massage once again.

"Ah."

Nobody was around this part of the beach, but I knew it wouldn't take long to reach the crowds in the distance. I remembered the position of our towels before the mad circumstances occurred. It worried me that Jason may have called for the life guards, or assumed my death. I needed to find him swiftly.

I ran, knowing that I had these new abilities, but that I couldn't activate them in public. I remember the alien saying that I would know how and when to activate my abilities in order to live a normal life here. It felt safe and reassuring to have this new knowledge.

I grew extremely close to the beach spot that Jason and I had picked.
It was surprising to see that our towels were still in the same position. I looked down to remember the strange towelling around my body! What if this was revolutionary material I was holding onto? Nobody would know anyway. It wasn't like someone would recognise it to be so strange that it needed to go to a laboratory! It just looked like a slightly different white towel.

I needed to activate my heightened senses to locate Jason. Now this was something I knew I could do without drawing attention to myself. I felt myself hone into Jason's energy somehow. Upon the honing in, I located him with my eyes. He was walking through the sand nearest the sea. I heard him shouting around to everyone he possibly could to get help.
He cared!
I think we had something special worth saving and he was one of the main reasons for my wishing to return. I prayed that this was a good decision. He looked amazing, running around with his perfect body despite the crazy panic he was in!
I ran over as swiftly as I could, trying to stop him running in all of the directions he was hysterically turning to.

"Jason! ... Jason!"

He heard my voice and turned his head, not expecting to see me running towards him. A second glance in my direction gave him his confirmation!

"Oh, you bloody idiot!" He shouted with a strong, booming voice.

They weren't the reactive words I expected.

"Why am I an idiot? I managed to get back to shore safely and couldn't find *you*!"

"What the hell? Where the hell did you get to? You swam off like a mad woman!"

We were now close enough to hear within normal range.

He grabbed me hard around my upper back and tucked his head into my shoulder.

"I'm so sorry I reacted so badly. I can't believe I frightened you off!"

I noted his hands feeling around for any strange things on my back.

"It's okay. It was just something that must have stuck to me that floated over."

"Wow! It must have been so sticky! It looked so freaky, like you had a fin! It freaked me out!"

I thought I would join in on the freaky bit.

"Well, it freaked me out too! I didn't know what the hell it was either, that's why I swam off so swiftly. I didn't know what it was and you were so shocked."

"I'm so sorry for the way I reacted. You feel like a normal woman now!" He giggled at the thought of his response.

"Do you really think humans can suddenly grow back blade things?" This was a terrible cover-up attempt.

He looked at me and grinned broadly.

"Certainly not!"

At least I knew it wouldn't be possible to discuss any personal alien changes with *him*!

Jason surprised me with his words after I fell into my own thoughts.

"So what are we going to do with the rest of our short moments we have here?"

"I guess we could just simply enjoy each other's company on the beach? Save any more potential disasters?"

"I think that's a damned fine idea." Jason smiled with his teeth and eyes. It was nice to see. "In fact, why don't we stay here until the later hours just to spread this out? I'm sure we'll be fine tomorrow morning for work. We're not the type to fall in on a Monday with a huge hangover, so a bit of tiredness wouldn't hurt for one day surely."

It was my time to smile broadly. He was beginning to relax more with me. It was great that he wanted to spend more time together.

"It's been a strange weekend," I added, "it's had a kind of 'stop-start' feel to it, but I'm sure when we are super familiar with each other, we'll thrive somehow. I think we're suited to each other."

Jason agreed with a mild nodding.

We were walking casually, hand in hand, back to our towels. Something really comforting really clicked with us. I wondered if *my* calm may have had a positive impact on things too.

The evening was beginning to draw in and some cool airflow worked its way over our bodies. We both placed warmer clothes over us and hugged with some loving kisses. It felt very romantic.

As we relaxed and had a wonderful sea view to admire, I spotted some surfers huddling together in the sea, some distance away. It occurred to me that Annie and her surfing crowd were gathering together for yet another one of their "adventures."
I decided to ignore them, since they had strange obsessions. With the decision on ignorance, I felt a strange tug on my chest. It was like a large rope had been attached to me somehow, wishing to reel me in. The feeling was slightly uncomfortable, but I tried to ignore it. We speak freely of "heart tugs", but this felt literal!
I threw a subtle glance at Jason and he was smiling with his eyes closed, facing the ball of sun. He was content for sure.
I ignored the tugging and attempted to relax in a similar manner. My eyes were closed and the gentle warmth of the evening sun was comfortable on my face. The discomfort in my chest continued however. It wasn't intense enough to feel pain, but it was still there.
"This is nice." I wanted to let Jason think that I was still comfortable, despite the constant tugging!
 "Mm, I'm in agreement with you there. Nothing can ruin this moment."

I was worried that something *could*!

I looked over at the usual group of surfers and wondered if they
were something like the head gang of this beach. The way they
behaved gave that impression. I really didn't want to interact
with them anymore. It was a huge mistake getting sucked into
their circle initially.
I noticed they were gaining distance on that same boat. I
wondered why they couldn't just let the old incident go; why they
couldn't just move on and let go.
The tug in my chest grew stronger, almost like someone was
pulling the rope harder. I felt myself move forward and pushed
back against it, trying hard to resist. I knew it was all relative to
what the surfers were doing. It was a strong pull towards that
particular scene.
Argh! What am I supposed to do?

The surfers were playing it cool, just hovering about the same zone
for ages. The tug continued and the sun dropped considerably. I
sensed Jason was soon to suggest departure, but I needed an excuse
to stay longer and observe.
"Can we stay a while longer? It's so romantic. There's no rush
just yet is there?"
Jason had a half-smile at this point.
"Oh, yeah, why not... We can stay as long as you like."
Phew!
I knew I could always use the toilet-hunting game again. It was
clear that I was going to move in on the surfers to interject

somehow. My body didn't really give me an option. I was a little confused though, as the alien said something about having control over my extra abilities, but this feeling was quite controlling! It wasn't the plan I had.

Darn you surfers!

I secretly monitored the gang's actions and held on now in complete darkness on the sand. I knew I was pushing it with Jason, so needed to give even further encouragement to stay. It felt ridiculous!

"Wow, this is so romantic in the dark, with the moon glowing on the water and the stars shining so clearly. Why don't we lie down and star gaze just for a while longer?"

Jason enjoyed this idea.

"Actually this is unique. How often can we say we gaze at the stars on the beach? ... In fact, we should move to the beach to do it in the summer every night."

Wow, I didn't expect him to be thinking that far ahead, but it was a good sign of present contentment.

Amazingly, I could see perfectly in the dark, focussing my eyes through, to see that one of the surfers was growing close to the side of the boat. The man was recognisable as the one with the smart Mohican hairstyle. He did seem to be the keener revenge-planner of the group. I noted his small backpack and his actions to remove an item that appeared to have a plastic covering. I tried to focus in further. It was so odd! My eyes were like amazing binoculars or some kind of double telescope! Either way I didn't want to change my thoughts to analytical ones at this time. I monitored his actions, feeling like this undercover police officer once again! This time I wanted to play things differently. I wanted to be a little more tactical about my actions.

The surfer held a brief conversation with others and then placed this item back into his backpack, strangely!

I wanted more view of the *item*, but I didn't have an opportunity. As soon as the surfer began climbing up the side of the boat I needed my toilet excuse!

"Hey Jase, I just need to find that loo again, okay?"

"In the dark, on your own? Let me come with you."

"Ah no, it's perfectly fine, I can see pretty well in the dark. I eat my carrots!" Light humour would surely help him to relax.

"Well okay, so long as you're back within ten minutes, otherwise I'll be hunting for you again. Don't leave me worrying!"

Gosh, was this my worried father?

"Don't worry! I'll be back before you know it. I'm desperate, so I need to rush."

"Rush along then, but please be cautious of weirdos."

"I can handle myself. I'll be back in a mojo!"

As I walked off, he still shouted words of caution and prompt actions!

I crept into the darkness and found a place to lay my warm clothes down.

It was easy to run into the sea water, diving into the deeper parts. My added abilities kicked in automatically and I swam comfortably and naturally. I was able to breathe with great rhythm, but with the strange breathing location being around my arm area again. I felt for my swimming attire and noticed all was in place!

The boat was so familiar yet again.

I swam to the opposite side as before, to creep up with my suction pads! All of this happened with automation again. The abilities were acting immediately upon the need of them, almost like the intention of muscle movement. I just needed the thought and intention to activate things.

It was easy to climb onto the boat and witness the next move. The surfer was moving with stealth. His Mohican hair was so prominent however. It was quite humorous to watch.

I noticed him crouch to remove the item from his bag yet again and unwrap the item from the plastic covering.

Not another bomb! It had the same features as the previous one. These surfers most certainly had some serious vengeance thing going on!

I observed the boat from inside, where I crouched down deeply, knowing somehow that I was blending into the colours of my surroundings like a Chameleon! This was understood now that my abilities were automatically clear to me!

A sudden realisation hit me! If I could blend in, then I was able to creep around without being noticed. So with this, I remained crouched, but moved swiftly around the boat, catching up with the surfer, managing to crawl within a meter of him. He sensed my presence though, I could tell! His head and eyes were looking around with paranoia. He aimed to place this bomb or dynamite package in a nearby cupboard. I assumed at this point that the owners of this boat were comfortably tucked in their beds in the upper parts. There were no signs of activity otherwise.

This surfer was doing a good sneaking job, that of Ninja level! I decided I needed to teach him a huge lesson. My idea would frighten the living daylights out of him, but it would hopefully solve this vengeance issue once and for all.

I touched his back and he spun around, letting out a gasp of fright. He looked around with panic, but obviously couldn't see me. I shifted to areas I knew would be easy to blend into. His panic calmed and he made his final moves to place this device into the cupboard. I could see that a timer was set for ten minutes. This was perfect for me! It was long enough for me to sort him out, as well as the background plan of not being too long for Jason!

He was just closing the cupboard nice and quietly now that everything was set perfectly for him.

I followed him as he crept quietly back towards the edge of the boat, where the ladder sat waiting for him.

Just as he was lifting a leg to climb over, I grabbed his leg. I heard a gasp of "Huh?" He must have initially assumed he'd been caught by the boat owners. His response was priceless. The panic in his face as he turned to see something of an outline of me was of such fear!

I knew I was camouflaged, but I could tell that a close eye would certainly see parts of my shape.

His face was that of the opposite expression of his usual cocky confidence. His eyes were large and his mouth was open with a downward pull, exposing his lower set of teeth. He leant backwards, naturally trying to pull away.

I laughed, a bit like a psychotic person in a horror film. I couldn't help it! It came out naturally!

He half-recognised me. I could tell by the change of focus in his eyes. His eyebrows lowered with confusion, but his words offered an explanation to himself.

"You?" He was frozen with fear now.

"Yes, me! Let's go for a swim! It's dark! Let's enjoy it!"

With that I pulled him back into the boat and dragged him over to the other side. I heard a mild gasp from the other surfers who were obviously monitoring his movements from below. They would only have seen him fall back onto the boat.

I pulled him with his leg to the opposite side of the boat and he screamed in a whisper, holding his awareness of the boat owners. My strength was beyond any human strength. There was no doubt that this would freak this man out completely! I pulled him over the edge of the boat, keeping a grip of him, now moving my hand down to his ankle. It must have really hurt his body, forcing him over the edge and landing him into the water. I noticed his hands and free leg trying to limit his injury with swift panic movements.

We were both in the sea now. I dragged him through the water, feeling as fast as a speedboat. He skimmed the surface of the water, trying to keep his head afloat. I had a plan to keep him intact, but give him the most frightening experience he could ever imagine. After a minute or two of extreme speed, I stopped with a great sharpness. Some alien blades seemed to expose themselves from me, like a set of brakes. I made sure this surfer's head was now above surface and looking directly at my face. He was catching his breath with heaviness, trying to focus through the sea water trickling down his face. We were both treading water, waiting for a moment of clarity. I wanted his full attention now. He stared at me.

"You bitch! What the hell are you doing?" He had his old, cocky expression back. His fighting spirit was now shining through.

He tried to grab my neck, but it was too thick with muscle for him to have any impact.

"What are you? We invited you into our group, you freak!"

"Oh yes, you invited me into your group with such kindness didn't you?"

He looked back at where the boat should be.

"You can't stop that bomb."

"Oh, but I can, and I did before... Why are you trying so hard to murder those poor people?"

"Poor people? They murdered a friend of ours. The police did jack shit! They deserve to die!"

The truth was forced and I didn't feel surprised.

"Well, it's not right to fight fire with fire. They will have their murder on their conscience. Isn't that enough? You don't want to have the same thing on your conscience for the rest of your life, do you? Knowing you've killed some people?"

"They killed my best buddy!" I noticed some tears flare up!

"How did he die?"

"They pushed him deep into the water and knocked him out. We weren't able to save him." He offered more detail without hesitation.

"Are you sure it wasn't an accident?"

"Are you insane? They are thieves. They've been stealing jewellery and selling it in private markets. They wanted to keep everyone away from their boat."

It all made sense, but I kind of guessed the most of it!

He started to attempt to swim away, but stopped after noticing the distance we were from everything.

This caused him to spin to face me again.

"What the hell are you?"

"I am here to stop this stupid behaviour."

"No... What the hell are you?"

He wanted answers.

"Look, I'll get rid of that boat if you promise to move forward and forget about all of this nonsense. Grieve your friend properly and then move on."

"How are you going to get rid of the boat? That bomb will be going off anyway."

"Just promise you'll stop this nonsense and I'll get you back to your friends and get the boat out of your sight forever."

I could tell he was growing tired now with the treading of water. His breath was getting heavier.

"You bitch! You complete bitch!"

"Thank you."

I swam closer to him and he panicked again.

"Get away from me! Get away you freak!"

I went under the water and grabbed one of his ankles again, dragging him under for a moment. I was aware of time now and pulled him faster than before. There was no way he would be able to control anything.

I dragged him back to the boat and spotted the empty surfboard that one of his friends was holding so patiently.

Coming to a halt, I pulled his head up to ensure he was conscious. He struggled for a few seconds, coughing and trying to locate his mind. His eyes were all over the place. I waited for a moment, holding him steady by his waist. His friend noticed him with such surprise and turned to offer hands of assistance.

"Are you okay mate?"

The Mohican surfer didn't respond. His mind was obviously all over the place. The speed of the water must have messed him up.

I felt slight pity for him over how he was grieving so badly, but taking the wrong actions in revenge. He obviously had some serious issues. I wondered if his friends were just in on this to support him.

I grabbed one of his hands now and placed it on the surfboard, keeping the connection until he gained some sort of awareness. His breathing calmed slightly.

When I could see that he had full support of his surfboard and friend, I swiftly moved onto the boat again, using the same side, knowing I was blending into the shades of colour.
I reached into the boat and crept to the cupboard swiftly. The timer was moving, giving me a sense of urgency. I grabbed this explosive with haste and ran to climb over the opposite side of the boat and back into the water.
My swimming speed took me beyond any distance I had experienced to this date!
I knew I was in foreign waters at this point. The timer reached its final minute, so I left it to slowly sink, as I swam just as swiftly back to the direction of the boat.

The bomb was so far out by the time I reached the proximity of the boat that it gave off such a light explosive noise, even to human ears! Everything was safe once again! Phew!
My next plan was to move the boat! I realised that Jason would be waiting for me, so I needed to do this very swiftly.
I dived deep into the water, reaching the area of the anchor.
This anchor appeared different to my childhood memory of them on television, but I was able to free it from the ground and swim back up with the weight in my arms. My feet pushed me up, back to the surface. I reached an edge of the boat and held the anchor

with one arm, whilst using my suction pads with one hand and two feet to climb my way up into the boat. This was a bizarre situation for sure!

Once the anchor was quietly placed over the edge, I submerged myself back into the water with an almost-silent dive. I found the back end of the boat and found the rudders. It was crazy how I could guide the boat with my swimming strength. I wasn't initially certain of this, but my mind visualised it, so I knew it was a possibility!

I pushed with great strength and speed. In the early stages, I witnessed the whispering words of the surfers, commenting on the movement. I pushed and pushed, creating momentum now.

I swam fast and hard with all of my might, thinking that I must be fairly far away now.

The distance I made was clear, when reaching another beach that was full of rocks and shells. I pushed the boat up onto the rough ground, enough to make it extremely difficult to push back out to sea.

I was curious on the location, so walked onto this land and ran with much speed again to see if there was any human life around. Thankfully I spotted a random house with lights on. I knocked on the door, automatically losing my alien features. An older man answered with a screwed-up feature of "what the hell are you doing knocking on my door at this hour?" He needed no words. I gave him innocent behaviour and told him that a boat was stranded on the shore and that they needed help. His expression changed to that of concern. He offered to make a call to the Coast Guard and with that I was able to leave with confidence.

I ran back down to the boat, noticing the people were franticly trying to figure out what had happened.
As I managed to climb back down, I noticed my feet were forming the strong webbed feature again. This explained the comfort when running bare footed! What a great element!

I reached the side of the boat and did something quite cruel. Then again I didn't know how "bad" these people were with the information I received. Maybe it was the karma they deserved. Thoughts on that aside, I went to the side of the boat, willing on my alien strength and hands. Once I noticed the change, I pushed a dent into the side of the boat. Following that, I ran over to the opposite side and tried to punch into the boat. Amazingly, I created a hole in the side, with my fist! This would need great repair! The noise I made created words of fuss on the boat. I needed to speed up yet again, but wanted to punch a few more holes into the side space just to ensure they'd be stranded for some time!
This was successful, despite the shocking noises from the voices above. They couldn't calculate this situation, so they were swearing frantically, moving around still trying to make sense of everything.

I looked on at my great work, pushing myself for time now. I relocated my direction for the return to Jason.

The swim I took on was ultra-fast once again! I could tell that I reached our original beach within a few short minutes!

The surfers were all huddling on the sand now, as I ran past them with my blended invisibility. I honed in with my ears to hear words of concern for the Mohican surfer. It was comforting to hear his responses. He was reassuring them that he was fine. I knew however that he must be aching badly! At the very least, he would be in pain from the dragging along the boat!

I ran back to find Jason sat upright, moving his head around. He spotted me and stood.
"I told you not to be long! You've left me worrying again!"
"I am so sorry!" I didn't seem to even need to get my breath back – amazing! "I needed a number two and it wasn't coming out easily!"
"Oh, lovely," He was obviously not wishing to hear that. "Can we go back to the car now? It's getting late."
The normality of his words were very strange to my ears.
"Yeah, I think it's time."
We packed our items up and carried everything back up to the car. I tried to shake the events from my mind with our peaceful walk.

The drive home was a relatively quiet one. I was lost within my thoughts of weirdness. The odd thing was that I was comfortable with the fact that I couldn't speak liberally about my strange, new life! Whilst having time to think, I did decide that I was going to protect Sue by telling her that all of my strange occurrences had ended. That way she can invent her own explanation for the events and it will all be something of the past. I hoped that after a day of the aliens putting everything into order for me, that I could live the normal Earthly life, however with enhanced abilities in my *secret* life.

Chapter Seven

Days had passed and I had put the record as straight as I could
with Sue; Jason and I were doing well and beginning to have
similar traits to those of an 'old married couple. I even visited the
"transportation device" a couple of times to learn more about
myself and get to know my new friends a little more. Shmea 3289
was actually quite a nervous, but sweet alien. I still wasn't sure
about the gender part of this alien community!

Frush67 never seemed to change his tone or emotion. I wasn't
sure if that would ever change, even as I grew closer to them.
I developed friendships with a couple of others on their planet.
The amazing colours and features of their lands were so
spectacular that it was enough to prompt a regular visit.
I even had a go in their strange vessels that blasted from one end of
their planet to another. I felt like I was on some Sci-Fi movie!
In fact the whole thing didn't seem real at any time of me visiting.
It was always a more wonderful feeling knowing that I was
returning home to Earth. I had certainly made the right decision.

Everything was fitting perfectly.
My life was completely different, but for the better. I felt uniquely
special, even though this entire situation was one big accident!

I loved my new social life with my female friends and our new friend, Justin. Sue bonded well with everyone and we decided to have our regular parties, but with quiet, tinny music! Since there was a compromise on preferences, I talked Patrick and his wife into joining in and he finally agreed to "let his hair down." Everyone had grown closer.

I preferred to see Jason in our private hours so that we could enjoy each other's company, as we should.

Work and routines settled perfectly with the occasional bit of spontaneity.

Today I decided on some personal spontaneity. It was the weekend and I chose to take a trip down to the beach for an outlet of my alien abilities! Jason was working, but the day was too beautiful to miss. I was drawn to the great waters.

I had a smooth journey down and parked up easily.
I carried the surfboard down with me, along with my bag of goods. The beach was packed with people! I spotted my perfect location between some single people sunbathing in peace. This time I chose to wear my full swimming costume to avoid any parts coming loose! It was too lovely for a wetsuit in my opinion. I could imagine some surfers disagreeing with me for some reason, since I didn't understand the sport to its full extent.

My patch of sea directly ahead was empty of any surf or body boarders, so I thought it would be good for space and liberal fun. First however, I was going to get some sun on my skin. Lying in the sun for a while would warm me up enough to want some cooling water.

I must have fallen asleep for a moment or two, as some people around me had already moved on, perhaps to grab a drink or food. The sea ahead of me looked lovely and clear. I flipped myself over, catching glimpse of all changes. Looking at the time, I noticed I must have drifted for a couple of hours! My skin didn't appear red or sore, so I felt relief with that.

A shadow came over me, forcing me to look up.

"Hello Jen!"

You are friggin' kidding me!

Not surprising – Annie was stood over me, hovering with her hair flopping forward perfectly. She was carrying her surfboard this time, fully kitted up with a wetsuit.

"Ah, how did you spot me?"

"I always spot you Jen. You stand out like a sore thumb."

She pointed to my surfboard. It did have a distinctive shape and the colours were vibrant in places. The first surfboard wasn't too dissimilar. I also had a habit of laying it at an angle, over my bag.

"Besides," she continued, "I do walk up this stretch of beach pretty much daily."

Now that made much more sense. Perhaps she was just making fun of my surfboard.

"So, you fancy doing a bit of surfing with me?" She offered.

"Well, I did have a plan to practice here in my own space."

"Okay, it's entirely up to you. I thought it would be nice to catch up. You didn't let me know you were coming. Anyone would begin to get a complex by now."

Shit, she is a real sticky one.

"Well every time I've been this way you've spotted me, so it's the only times I've been. I wanted to get more confident with surfing before joining in with anyone else. How is everyone anyway?"

"Why don't you come and see for yourself later on? We're having our usual get-together later if you fancy it?"

Gosh, this was getting to be like a stuck record.

"Ah, you know what Annie? I think I'll give it a miss. I've got a plan to head back for a romantic meal this evening."

"Okay, well I take that as a hint. I'm not going to grovel for your friendship."

Ah shit. This was turning into an awkward one!

Thankfully Annie walked off without further word. She had a way of making me feel guilty.

Since she was in eye view, I realised this was an opportunity to catch sight of her gang!

Of course! My honing in skills!

She walked for quite a while, appearing to look for more victims to pester.

A sense of loss came over me, followed shortly by relief. I didn't *actually* lose a friend. The good thing was that she pulled me into a situation where I could save a bunch of people from murder!

Losing my track of her for a moment, I glanced out to sea, to notice no view of any anchored boats. I was confident about my crazy resolving methods however!

I felt I knew that Annie wouldn't pester me anymore. I found her with my eyes again. She walked with such confidence. Her strut took her to a few members of her usual crowd. I recognised some of the figures. I zoned in with my strange eye abilities and tried to identify each one. Everyone looked happy and full of laughs. It was lovely to see. I noted one man who looked unrecognisable for a moment. He had dark, floppy hair and relaxed features. Perhaps it was a new member they'd managed to lure in. I was just about to look away when I recognised a distinctive mark! The man I didn't recognise was "Mohican Man"! His Mohican had dropped and his features were relaxed! I studied him again, this time with more intensity. It was most definitely him! He had moved on! The smile on his face was authentic. The creases in the corner of his eyes were of genuine happiness! Wow! He recovered fast! Didn't I freak him out at all? Did he receive some kind of administration of happiness? With that, a thought crossed my mind. It couldn't be! I looked down at the palm of my hands and willed them into their alien state. As I did, extremely tiny, yet striking lights shone from my palms! Did I administer happiness? Wow! I didn't even think about *that* ability!

My job here is done!

The group of surfers grew larger and I recognised all of the members clearly now. Everything looked happy and settled. It was nice to view them from afar without any connection. Hopefully they will remain contented for many years to come.

I wanted to head into the water for a cooling session, but sat for a while longer, feeling as if I needed a little reflection time on everything that had happened in the last few weeks. It all began with a desire to have a little more fun!
One lesson was for sure… "Be careful what you wish for!"

After a few moments, I grabbed my surfboard and thought I'd better do the "waxing" job. As I waxed my board I noted a little fuss in the water, directly in my eye line. Two men were fighting over something. It turned into a bit of a fist fight. One man looked as if he lost consciousness with a connecting fist and crash landed into the depths of the sea water. The other man swam away swiftly, almost as if he planned to leave this person for death! My automatic movements were to run drastically to rescue this man. I ran fast on the sand and into the shallow water, diving deeper in for the rescue. My webbed fingers and toes stretched out and pushed my actions into hyper speed! I saw the man floating down lifeless. My duty was to save him! I knew I could and I most certainly will!
Here we go again…!

This is my life...
I accept it.
This is my purpose.
Life will never be the same again!
I am a weird, alien superwoman!
I am Jelly!

End

Emma Jayne Taylor

Twitter: @emmalini333

Website: www.ejtbooks.com

Printed in Great Britain
by Amazon